MERCILESS

KRISTAL STITTLE

Encyclopocalypse Publications
www.encyclopocalypse.com

To Sammy and Tyler
For getting me out of the house

CHAPTER ONE

MERCY WAS HAPPY TO finally be home from work; it had been a long day on the coma ward. There had been a fairly bad bus accident within the Callus General Hospital's district, so all the injured had been sent to them. This meant the ER was constantly short on beds and kept pestering the coma ward to allow them to use some of their empty ones. Everyone always called the coma ward first when they were short on beds. As a nurse, Mercy had to keep track of where all their equipment and patients were, on top of her regular care duties.

One of their patients had even miraculously woken up today after a five-year "sleep." Although that was always an exciting and happy moment, it was a lot of work. They had to bring the patient up-to-speed about had what happened to him, mediate family visits, constantly check on vitals to make sure the patient wasn't going to have a relapse, fill out a ton of paperwork, and, for those who had been under a long time, begin the extensive physiotherapy process as well as the testing of mental functions. It could take weeks, even months, to get the patient strong enough just to get out of his bed on his own.

Upon entering her apartment, Mercy hung up her light spring jacket in the closet, and took off her running shoes. She felt disappointed that Roofus wasn't there to greet her. The fluffy Chou Chou had gone north with her boyfriend on a males-only fishing weekend. Heading into the kitchen, Mercy turned on the coffee machine and within minutes delighted at the delicious aroma. She had always loved the smell of coffee ever since she had been a little girl. Her dad would have at least three cups a day out of a big black mug that said *kan ta ca ye* on the side. Neither of them had ever learned what those words really meant, but they also hadn't put much effort into finding out. Not knowing made them magical.

As she waited for her coffee, Mercy decided to check the home phone for messages. She didn't have many friends, but people did try to call her from time to time, and she was always forgetting to unsilence her cell, so they'd try here. It was usually her mom. And Kenny may have called to leave a message about how the trip was going so far. The voicemail service told her that she had five messages waiting, a new record.

The first message *was* from her mom. She wanted to know if Mercy could come an hour early to their family's regular Sunday dinner. This didn't surprise Mercy as her brother, Tom, and his wife just had a baby, and needed to eat earlier to keep to the baby's schedule. Mercy made a mental note to call her mom back and say that it was fine.

The second message was not so cheery. At first, there was nothing but dead air. That sometimes happened when the voicemail service malfunctioned, and whoever was calling hadn't realized that it had picked up. But then came the heavy breathing. Mercy couldn't identify who it was, but cold chills ran up and down her spine. Something about it seemed so menacing. Mercy was tempted to stop the playback, but didn't. She stood there, feeling a vague, cold terror, just letting it run. Then a voice spoke one word.

"Mercy," it whispered in a smooth, barely audible voice.

Mercy's blood froze. Something deep inside her told her that the mystery caller over the line wasn't asking for mercy, but was saying her name.

The click of the phone hanging up echoed loudly inside Mercy's ear. She was gripping the handset with white knuckles, the phone pressed against the side of her head so hard that it started to hurt. The machine's voice told her the message was over, and began relaying instructions about what she could do with it. Mercy pressed the delete button and hung up the phone. Although she couldn't say what had truly frightened her, it had gotten deep enough under her skin to make her hold off on listening to the other three messages.

Trying to shake off the call and forget that it had ever happened, Mercy went into the bathroom and took a quick, hot shower. Normally she would have loved to take a long, luxurious shower after work, but because of the message, she didn't feel comfortable being naked for too long. Her sister made fun of her for always being so jumpy, but it wasn't exactly something she could help being. Afterwards, she left her scrubs on the floor, and put on a pair of comfy track pants and a loose T-shirt. The coffee had finished brewing and so Mercy poured herself a big mug. It wasn't as big as her dad's had been but it was the closest she had been able to find.

With her hair still wrapped up in a towel, she looked at her phone again, where the message light continued to blink.

It was probably just one of her friends goofing around. They knew she was home alone this weekend, that her live-in boyfriend, Kenny, was up north. They were probably just trying to mess with her. In fact, it could have been Kenny himself; he wasn't above a juvenile joke or two. One of the other messages was probably from him, laughing, and then telling Mercy that he had gotten to the cabin safely. Mercy convinced herself of this.

With her mug in hand, she sat down in the over-stuffed reading chair that was right next to the phone. She picked it up out of its cradle and dialed the message service again.

The third message was not from Kenny like Mercy had expected. It didn't seem to be from anyone actually. It was one of those annoying messages where the caller hung up right after the message started recording. It was swiftly deleted.

Message four began playing. More breathing. This time it was different, though. The other message had had a slow, smooth sound to it, but this time it was quick, panicked, even ragged. Mercy thought that maybe the first breather had been breathing through his nose, whereas this time she suspected it was coming from a mouth. It reminded Mercy of Roofus. Now that she thought about it, it probably *was* Roofus. More of Kenny being an ass.

As her finger hovered over the delete button, the sound changed. There was a quick tearing, and then a gargling sound. Only it wasn't really gargling. Mercy's nurse training told her it was the sound of someone choking, likely on some sort of liquid. Her hands started shaking but she steeled her nerves and stopped them. When the message ended, she decided not to delete it. If it *was* from Kenny, she was going to play it for him when he got back, and explain to him how unfunny it was.

The final message was from her mom again. She was saying something about changing the Sunday menu due to some diet Tom had apparently just started. Mercy only half listened as she continued thinking about the previous message. The choking really wasn't funny, not even a little bit.

Cutting off the tail end of her mother's message, Mercy opened the phone line to make a call, the dial tone monotonously whining. She held her finger over the 9 button, fully intending to call 9-1-1, but then stopped herself. She couldn't be sure of what she had heard. And it really could have just been someone taking a joke too far.

Mercy dialed Kenny's cell phone. She was going to tell him his joke wasn't funny, and that it had upset her. If he confessed, she would forgive him, but only after making sure he knew how badly he had scared her. She would smother him with guilt over it.

If it turned out that it wasn't Kenny playing a joke, then she'd ask his advice about what to do. Maybe even go over to her friend Joanna's place for the night; she wouldn't mind the company. A month ago, Joanna's husband had left her for a younger woman. She wasn't terribly crushed, they had a lot of other problems, but she took up all offers to be with friends.

The phone rang and rang. Finally Kenny's voicemail picked up. Mercy left a message telling him he wasn't funny, and that she'd try again in case he had just missed the call. She actually tried two more times with no answer. When she was about to try a fourth time, the phone rang in her hand, startling her. She hit the connect button, barely noticing that it was Kenny's number on the call display, and held the phone tightly to her ear.

"Kenny?" her voice had more worry in it than she had intended.

"Hey, Mercy, it's John," one of Kenny's friends answered. "Kenny's driving."

"You're not at the cabin yet?"

"No, Sheppard took us on some crazy detour, insisting we try out some restaurant on the way. You okay?"

"Yeah. Yeah, I'm fine."

"Sorry it took so long to get back to you. Kenny's phone was buried in his bag, and it took us awhile to dig it out."

"Neither of you guys called earlier did you? Left a couple of voice-mails?"

"No. Why? Something wrong?"

Mercy could hear Kenny in the background, asking what was up. Just hearing his voice, even at a fuzzy distance, put Mercy at ease.

"I just had some odd messages. Heavy breathing kind of stuff. I thought maybe you guys were playing some sort of mean joke."

"Not us. Sorry. Maybe they just got a wrong number?"

Mercy hadn't thought about that. Their landline got quite a few wrong numbers. Maybe whoever had called just hadn't picked up on the fact that it was a wrong number after listening to the voicemail message. She could have been mistaken about hearing her own name.

"Could be that," Mercy agreed, glad that there was a rational explanation. "Or maybe just some punk kids, making random prank calls."

"Yeah, kids these days can be assholes."

"Thanks, John."

"No problem. Although if it persists, call me or Kenny. We could probably get someone from the precinct to trace the call and put a little fear into whoever it is."

"Sounds good." Mercy found herself smiling. Kenny and John were partners in law enforcement. Mostly they just wrote out traffic tickets to people, or directed cars when the lights at an intersection went out, but they knew a lot of detectives and even some SWAT guys. Having the chance to intimidate some punks would probably make their day.

"Take care of yourself."

"You, too. And take care of Kenny and Roofus while you're at it. Lord knows the two of them need looking after."

John laughed. "I'll tell him you said that."

"Bye, John."

"Bye, Mercy."

Mercy hung up her phone. She felt a lot better having spoken to someone. Although Mercy wouldn't describe herself as creative, her imagination did carry her off from time to time. She couldn't stand to watch a movie that was even remotely scary, because then that night she wouldn't be able to sleep, thinking something awful was going to happen to her. Kenny preferred those kinds of movies to Mercy's collection of rom-coms, but he was a sweetheart and put up with them. Besides, if she was up all night, scared of something being under the bed, then Kenny had to stay up all night too, trying to make her feel safe.

Thinking of movies, Mercy decided to put one on while she dried her hair and cooked dinner. She loved her apartment's layout. A pass-through in the wall between the kitchen and the living room allowed her to see Kenny's big, flat-screen TV while she was in the kitchen. The flat-screen was probably the most modern thing in their living room. All of their furniture was cobbled together from things their older siblings or parents had decided to dispose of. The maroon, over-stuffed reading chair, which was Mercy's favourite, had originally belonged to her grandparents. There was also a beige couch, two faded green wingbacks next to the window, and a squat, banged-up, wooden coffee table that had once belonged to various members of Kenny's family. The super-plushy gray rug that filled most of the living room, the standing lamps, and the TV stand had come from Mercy's family. The shelves lining the room were the only things that they had bought together. Every space that could hold a shelf had one, and they were stuffed with Kenny's massive movie and video game collection, alongside Mercy's many books. The room had an awfully unmatched look to it, but neither Kenny nor Mercy minded at all. It was their favourite place to be.

The kitchen wasn't much better. The appliances came from different decades, and she was hard-pressed to find two dishes that matched. Coming from families with multiple siblings and having gone through periods of being poor as children, meant a lot of stuff got passed around and reused. Both Mercy and Kenny had been brought up with the belief that everything broken could be fixed, and nothing should go to waste.

With that in mind, Mercy carefully picked out her meal. She didn't want to make more than she could eat. Kenny wasn't averse to putting leftovers into the fridge, but Mercy wasn't a big fan of reheated food. If she could eat fresh, she would.

As the movie continued playing in the living room, Mercy began cooking dinner. It was a simple meal, consisting of a broiled chicken breast, a small Caesar salad, a fried pepper, and French fries. Normally, Mercy would really cook up a storm, using spices, all sorts of fruits and vegetables, home-made pastes and bastes, oils, whatever she could think of. Her mom had instilled a healthy love of cooking in her daughters. Even Mercy's sister, Faith, who was away at college and surrounded by quick, fried foods, would cook her own meals every chance she got.

Once the food was ready and the pots and pans were soaking in the sink, Mercy curled up on the couch with her plate to finish the film. It was a nice, quiet way to wind down from a hectic Friday. From a hectic week, actually. Now she had the next two days off to spend at home alone, without even the dog to take care of.

She was pretty sure she would go insane with boredom.

CHAPTER TWO

MERCY WAS FINALLY GETTING things done that she had been putting off for too long. First thing Saturday morning she went through all her clothes, separating those that she either didn't wear anymore or that were too small. The not-wearable pile was then put into plastic garbage bags, which she would take to her parents' place on Sunday. From there, her mom, her sister, and her sister-in-law would go through the clothes, picking out the ones they liked and that fit. Anything not chosen would be given to Goodwill.

Afterward, she stitched up any holes that were in her remaining clothes, and went through Kenny's to do the same. There were a lot of Kenny's clothes she'd like to get rid of, but she wouldn't do that to him while he was away. She did make a mental note to badger him about a few particular items when he got back, however.

With the clothes taken care of, and a load of laundry started, Mercy moved on to dusting. Although she ran a duster around the place at least once a month, she had been intending to get a more thorough cleaning done for quite some time. She pulled things off the shelves, wiping them down, and running some polish across the surface underneath. In the bedroom there was a swarm of Mercy's knickknacks to clean, and in the office was an army of Kenny's collectable toys and figurines. She even rearranged a bunch of them to display the items better.

Once the dust was gone, Mercy realized how dirty the lower sections of her walls were. Roofus loved mud puddles. Although they cleaned him as best they could and confined him to the front hall when he got messy, he still tracked a lot of dirt around the place. Not to mention his shedding. With her cleaning rag in one hand and her spray bottle in the other, Mercy set to work on the walls.

It was just as she was finishing up this latest job that the phone rang. Throwing her rag over the shoulder of her housework shirt, she left the spray bottle on the floor and crossed the room to the phone. Everything was starting to smell like oranges, a scent that Mercy liked almost as much as coffee. If a cleaning supply had an orange depicted on the label, Mercy bought it.

"Hello?" she answered cheerily the moment the handset was pressed to her ear.

Silence greeted her.

"Hello?" she said again, this time with confusion and annoyance in her voice.

Heavy breathing. It was just like the first message she had gotten the night before.

"Ha ha," Mercy told the caller, unamused. "You know my boyfriend is a cop? You keep crank-calling me like this and I'm going to have him and his cop friends find you."

Just more breathing. Mercy was determined to wait it out. Now that she was well rested and not fresh off a nightmarish shift, the breathing didn't seem as frightening. Still, there was a menacing quality to it that continued to concern her.

"Mercy," the voice—a man's voice—hissed.

She had managed to convince herself that the man hadn't said her name on the voicemail the day before. To hear it now, chilled her to the core. This time Mercy's silence was brought on by a lack of voice rather than a will to stay silent.

"Mercy Chalmers," that smooth voice spoke again.

There was no denying now that the speaker knew Mercy's name rather than having just used a coincidental word. Mercy slammed the phone back down on its cradle. Her hands were steady because her entire body had gone completely rigid. She stood as still as a statue, her hand still pressing down on the phone, her eyes glued to the little display window.

With sudden movements like that of a bird, Mercy's hand darted to the buttons next to the display window. She pressed the left button, which would bring up the last number to call here. It simply read Unknown Name, Unknown Number. It wasn't the first number like that to have called the landline, but it was the first that had come across as threatening rather than trying to sell something.

Still moving with sharp and sudden actions, Mercy located her cell phone on its charger. She called Kenny's cell with it, not wanting to change the last number on the home line. Kenny didn't pick up and it went to his voicemail. Hearing his recorded voice wasn't as calming as the real thing, but it settled her nerves enough to let her relay what had happened in a logical and almost calm manner. She hadn't really thought that Kenny would pick up, but she had hoped he would. The guys usually turned their phones off or left them in the cabin while they were out on the lake. Something about the ringers and vibrators scaring away all the big fish.

With the message left, there wasn't much else Mercy could think of doing about the situation. It was in Kenny's hands now, and he would handle it accordingly.

She returned to cleaning the apartment. Although scrubbing the walls hadn't seemed like such a chore before, her heart was no longer in it. Still, she persisted in doing all the things she had planned to do. She wasn't going to let the call ruin her day, although really, it already had.

It was after nightfall, while Mercy was having a bubble bath with a good book held above the water line that her cell phone went off. Since she had been waiting for Kenny to call her back, she had brought her phone into the bathroom with her. Reaching down, she picked the device up off the floor and looked at the display. Normally, Mercy would answer her phone right away, but even though the creepy calls had only come to the home line so far, she checked to make sure that it was Kenny.

"Hey, babe," she answered, glad that it wasn't an unknown number.

"Hey, I just got your message. You okay?"

Although Mercy had explained everything to his voicemail, she went over it again with him.

"So no actual threats have been made?"

"No."

"Okay, that's good. I don't like it, but it's better than a flat-out threat. I'll call some guys and get them to track down the number that called you. Some people owe me a few favours."

"Thanks, Kenny."

"Do you want me to come home? If I leave now, I could be there before sun-up."

"No, no. Don't do that." Mercy didn't want her boyfriend to risk falling asleep at the wheel and becoming a splatter at the side of the road.

"You sure?"

"Yes. You enjoy your trip," she insisted. "If I get scared, I'll invite Joanna over."

"Okay. You'll call me if anything else happens, right?"

"Of course, right away."

"I'll keep my phone on me this time."

Their conversation slowly shifted off the distasteful topic, and Kenny began telling Mercy how the trip was going so far. Apparently not great on the fish front, as they had only caught a few small fries that they threw back, but the boys' trips were never about the fish, and so they were having a fantastic time. According to Kenny, Roofus loved the woods. If he wasn't chasing squirrels through the trees, he was lounging in a sunny spot on the front porch. Kenny's friend, Sheppard, had brought his little Cocker Spaniel along and the two dogs had become fast friends.

When the conversation finally ended, mostly thanks to badgering from Kenny's buddies, Mercy was back to the happy mood in which she had started her day. She ended her bath feeling a lot more relaxed than when she had started it and got out only when the water became too cold.

Snuggling under the bed covers in one of Kenny's shirts, Mercy continued to read her book. It had been written for teenagers, but she liked the simple read about adventure and sexual frustration. Recalling her own teenage years, there was always at least one character she could relate to in these kinds of books.

When, at last, her light was turned out, Mercy's cell phone was sitting on the bedside table. The charger for her phone was in the living room but she'd been too tired to fight with the shelving unit blocking the outlet into which the charger was plugged. She wanted her phone close by, just in case Kenny had to call her about something important, like an officer needing to stop by to look at the phone. That, or, God forbid, she had to call him about something more important.

Her imagination caused her to worry about the windows, despite being eight stories up.

CHAPTER THREE

All Sunday morning, Mercy busied herself around the apartment. She did things that didn't really need doing, like mopping the balcony and washing the windows. She even reordered a stack of her mismatched plates so that they weren't so precariously balanced.

She was looking forward to going to her parents' today. Although she always looked forward to it, after her hard week and those creepy calls, it would be extra nice to go to her childhood home. Not to mention the fact that she loved seeing Tom's new baby. Mercy had fallen in love with her nephew the moment she had laid eyes on him three weeks ago. She looked forward to asking how things were going, especially now that her brother's two weeks off were up, and he had returned to work.

On a normal Sunday, Mercy would leave the apartment in time to arrive around 4 p.m., but on this Sunday she left half an hour earlier. It was good to get out and go for a drive.

The drive to the Chalmers family home was always a nice one. Mercy expertly navigated the city side streets, avoiding major, jammed-up routes, and long traffic lights. Just outside the city was a well-maintained suburban area, and then a larger suburban area still under development. Past that was nothing but farm lands. Mercy loved the open spaces, the quiet, and the solitude. Growing up, she could jog for miles without bumping into any cars or other people on the roads. The farmhouse had belonged to her mother's family. Mercy's grandfather had run a sheep farm and also owned a large chunk of the nearby woods. After her grandmother had passed, before Mercy was born, Mercy's mother had moved back into the house to help out her grandfather. When he passed as well, when Mercy was eight, the house had been given to her mother. That's when their poor period had started. Mercy's mother and father didn't understand the nuances of sheep farming. Without anything else to fall back on, they started to become strapped for cash. It was then that the sheep, along with their grazing land, were sold off to their neighbour. They got a good price for them, and knew the sheep would be well taken care of. They held onto the woods though. According to her dad, they kept the woods for Mercy and her siblings. If anything awful happened, and they needed a lot of money in a reasonable amount of time, the logging companies would snap up those trees in a heartbeat. Mercy wasn't even sure how much land they actually owned; just that it was a substantial amount. Eventually, her dad's screenwriting took off, even earning him an Academy Award, and they started to be flooded with cash; at least when compared to what they were used to. Just in time too, as Tom had been stressing over how to pay for college or university, and Mercy wasn't far behind.

As she drove down the small roads between the cow pastures she knew so well, all her cares slid away. They had become what her grandfather called 'city problems'. None of those issues could touch her while she was in the country. She was feeling so good that she turned off her little car's air conditioner and rolled down the window. It was a beautiful, sunny, spring day. The last few days had been a touch cool, which was usual for this time of year, but today was special. The temperature was up around 23 degrees Celsius, which was perfect in Mercy's opinion. The breeze through the car window was gentle, buffeting her shoulder-length hair against her cheeks. At this time of year, her hair was still a shade darker than blond, but by midsummer it would be golden. Her mom called it her magical hair, which she had gotten from her father. Her eyes were all her mother's though: a deep, honey brown. Mercy thought of herself as pretty, but not beautiful like her sister, Faith. She thought her facial features were too plain. Her nose was slightly bent, and she didn't really like the beauty mark next to her left eye. Still, she would never consider corrective surgery, and didn't try to hide herself under pounds of makeup. Having Kenny constantly telling her how beautiful she was in his own eyes, always helped to reaffirm those choices.

As Mercy turned onto her parents' road, meaning she was only a few minutes away, her cell phone rang. She pressed the button on the side of her hands-free device to answer it.

"Hello?"

"Mercy? It's mom." She sounded stressed out. "Where are you?"

"I just turned onto the road, why? What's wrong?"

"It's Robin. Tom and Emily are taking him to the hospital." Mercy's mom was practically hysterical.

Mercy pulled over to the side of the road, not trusting her judgment after hearing such words. Robin was her newborn nephew.

"Apparently he started gasping just as they were getting ready to leave."

"Mom, calm down." Mercy could barely remain calm herself. "What are you doing right now?"

"Driving to the hospital to meet them."

"You shouldn't be driving in your state, especially if you're on the phone." Mercy knew her mother didn't own a hands-free device.

"No, no, your father is driving us."

"Good. Remember to take deep breaths. I'm sure everything will be okay." Although her own stomach had cramped tightly, she focused on saying what her mother needed to hear. When Mercy had first become a nurse, she had started out in the ER. Just one blue baby had been enough for her to know that she couldn't work there and had requested a transfer. It had taken a few agonizing months, but she had eventually been moved to the coma ward, which was one of the best in the country and was what the hospital was best known for. It was far better suited to Mercy.

Over the phone, her mom made a series of unformed sounds and words. She needed to say something, but didn't know what to say.

"Deep breaths, Mom," Mercy repeated.

"I think I left the stove on. But we're already twenty minutes out. The house could burn down!"

Mercy could hear her dad attempting to soothe her mother from the driver's seat. Her mom started arguing with him, and with herself, about what to do.

"Mom," Mercy tried to get her attention but she wasn't listening. "Mom!"

The woman fell silent.

"I'm not far from the house. I'll go and turn the stove off. You get to the hospital and provide support for Tom and Emily, I'm sure they'll need it." Although Mercy's mother had no problem freaking out to her children, she had the ability to become a rock for them when their own stress was higher.

"The food's not ready yet, and I don't know how long we'll be." Her only grandchild was being rushed to the hospital, and still she found room in her heart to worry about not having food prepared for another of her offspring.

"That's all right. I can make my own food. In fact, if nothing's too burnt, I'll save what you started. We can reheat it later if we have to."

"Are you sure?"

"Yes, I'm sure, Mom. Just focus on the others."

"Okay. I'll call you when I hear more information."

"All right. Should I call Faith?" Faith was attending University several cities over, studying to become an actress. She had the looks, Mercy thought she had the talent, and their dad had connections, so she had a decent chance of at least making a living at it. Still, as a backup, Faith was also majoring in English, and would be taking a teaching course. It seemed to Mercy that everybody had 'teacher' as their backup.

"No, she has exams coming up. She'll be studying and rehearsing like crazy. There's no need to bother her yet." Mercy's mother was finally calming down. Talking things out always helped her.

"All right."

"I'll call her afterward so that she's up-to-date."

Neither of the women on the phone entertained the idea of the worst case scenario.

"Okay. I should hang up now and get to the house. If you need anything brought from home, just call and I'll drive it out." Mercy's stomach had unclenched a little now that her mom was calm.

"You don't need to do that, but thank you."

"Bye, Mom."

"Call you later, Mercy dear."

When Mercy hung up the phone, she continued to sit by the side of the road for awhile longer. Her hands trembled slightly against the rubberized plastic of her steering wheel. After about five minutes, she managed to reel in her distress and put the car in drive. She continued down the road to her parents' place, doing her best not to think about her baby nephew.

Within moments she had reached the neighbours' place. Mrs. Abram, the wife of Mr. Abram, the sheep farmer, was near the end of her driveway. She looked up as Mercy's car approached, because a car on this road was unusual. She recognized Mercy right away and flagged her down. Mercy pulled over for the second time and rolled down her passenger side window.

"Hello, Mrs. Abram."

"Hello, Mercy." The old woman leaned in through the window. Although elderly, she and her husband were still quite fit and spry, managing their farm mostly by themselves. "I saw your mother and father go racing past earlier. Is everything all right?"

Mercy relayed what little information she had, making sure to word it in such a way that it didn't sound too bad.

"Oh my, I hope the little darling is okay."

"I'm sure he will be." Again, Mercy had no idea, but she had to believe what she said.

"Well, keep me informed."

"I will." The Abrams had lived down the road from the Chalmers since Mercy's grandfather's days. The two families had always been very close, and were practically relatives themselves.

Mercy and Mrs. Abram exchanged a few more pleasantries, and then Mercy headed on up the road again.

After another minute of driving past nothing but sheep-grazing land, the Chalmers' home came into view. It was a lovely two-storey made of solid dark wood. The many windows were trimmed in white, as was the front door. The large front and back porches were also lined in white and decorated with white Muskoka chairs and a porch swing. Even in the middle of the day, several windows glowed cheerily from the lights that had been left on inside. The house was very old, with an odd layout of rooms and hallways. There were even secret passages in some of the rooms, which had delighted Mercy growing up. No one knew why the passages had been built, but they had always been there. They were even harder to find now that Mercy's father had spent quite a bit of money sprucing up the house. He was very careful, however, not to change its overall design and homey feel while renovating.

Mercy drove her little car, which she had bought used, up the gravel driveway. On the right side of the driveway, the side toward the Abrams', was a fence that traveled far beyond the house, where it disappeared over the hill. This was the edge of the sheep-grazing land, and currently, a few of the not-quite-white animals were hanging around. On the other side of the house was a small field that ended at the edge of their woods. The woods went on farther than Mercy had managed to explore as a child. There were no other houses or farms in that direction. As the road met the woods, it turned into a series of unnamed dirt trails that wound through the trees in nonsensical directions. Several people in the area, Mercy's brother included, often drove four-wheelers down them. And a handful, again, Mercy's brother included, had even gotten lost, and had taken hours to find their way back.

After parking as close to the door as the driveway allowed, Mercy rolled up her windows and turned off her car. She really didn't need to lock the doors out in the country, but she did so out of habit. First she took out her spring coat, however. Although it was still warm enough to continue wearing just her green sundress, she figured that the sun would be down by the time she left and that it would be colder. The bags of clothes she was getting rid of were in the trunk, but she decided to leave them there for now. Her mom could go through them another time.

As Mercy had expected, the door to the house was unlocked. She let herself in, hanging her jacket on a coat rack next to the door and slipping out of her sneakers. Mercy breathed deeply, taking in the scent she always associated with the earlier years of her life. In spite of all the work that had been done, the house remained the same. Her father had replaced all the wood in the walls on the first floor, which had been slowly warping and even rotting, but he made sure to stain the new wood the same old shade: a golden brown, like a perfectly toasted marshmallow. The floor in the front hall was carefully-cut stone that had been laid together and smoothed flat. As Mercy moved deeper into the house, the floor became a dark hardwood that matched the exterior. All the lighting came from beautiful, wrought-iron ceiling fixtures, some of which were the originals that had just been cleaned, fixed, and spruced up, while others had been custom-made to perfectly match. They hung from high, wood-panelled ceilings. To reach the kitchen, Mercy had to pass through the living room. It was laid out with pale, leather furniture circling a large red and white rug. One wall of the room had a large stone fireplace set into it. The stones matched the ones used in the front hall. On the walls hung photographs of flowers and fields that her mother had taken over the years. Although she never got serious about her photography, it was just a hobby for her, she did have a fairly good eye for composition, colour, and light. On wooden sideboards against the walls sat photos of the family throughout the years.

The living room was adjacent to the dining room, and from there, it connected to the kitchen.

In the kitchen, the cupboards and cabinets carried out the toasted-wood colouring, while the walls were white tiles, and the floor was more cut, grey stone. The appliances were all a slick black, the biggest change from the dingy yellow and off-white colours of Mercy's childhood. On the stove, a pot of water boiled furiously, occasionally spilling over and hissing against the flattop burner, leaving stains. Mercy turned off the stove and moved the pot. When she figured out what her mom had intended to use it for, she would start again. Next, she turned on the oven light and looked through the little window. A roast was slowly cooking inside, unharmed by the lack of supervision. Searching around the rest of the kitchen, Mercy determined that her mother was cooking roast, with mashed potatoes and corn on the side, a fruit salad appetizer, and pudding already finished and waiting in the fridge. Unless Tom was on the strangest diet Mercy had ever heard of, her mom had forgotten that she had changed the menu. Continuing to cook her mom's food helped take Mercy's mind off of Robin. She focused solely on doing her mother's meal the justice it deserved. When done, Mercy wasn't at all hungry. She filled in the time by dressing up equal portions on five plates, putting them in the warming drawer, and packing up everything else into Tupperware containers, which went into the fridge. With that done, she started washing all the dishes by hand, followed by drying and putting them away.

With nothing left to do, Mercy went back into the dining room and sat at the table, her hands tightly clasped in front of her. The room was similar in colour to the living room attached to it, with a large table in the center surrounded by high-backed dining chairs. The light hanging from the ceiling above the table matched those around the rest of the ground floor, but was even more ornate and chandelier-like. As Mercy sat at the table, she looked at the pair of family photos hanging on the wall opposite her. The first was an old picture, taken while her grandpa was still alive. It had been taken when Mercy was five years old, her sister just a newborn at the time. She stood to one side of her mother, who was sitting and holding her baby sister. Tom was on the other side, while her dad and grandpa stood behind everyone. It was a nice photo in which Mercy was grinning from ear to ear, the gap she used to have in her front teeth showing clearly. The other photo on the wall was more modern, taken only last year. Mercy's mom and dad stood in the middle, with Tom and Emily on one side, and Mercy, Kenny, and Faith on the other. Every time Mercy looked at the picture, all she could remember was how awkward the photo session had been, what with the photographer directing them and all the fake smiles. She wondered if that feeling would pass or if she would always see the photo as awkward.

When she focused on Tom and Emily in the picture, she started thinking about them being in the hospital with Robin. Mercy rose to her feet and left the dining room, heading into the living room so that she could pace on the rug. The pacing did little to calm her down, but it was better than sitting.

The cell phone in Mercy's jacket pocket started ringing, a loud sound in the quiet and empty house. She startled, then rushed to the front door, fighting her pocket momentarily, and then flipping open the device.

"Hello?"

Silence.

"Hello? Mom?" Sometimes her mom's cell phone had trouble connecting, and Mercy knew that some hospitals had signal dampeners to reduce the use of cell phones in the buildings.

Still silence.

"Mom, if you're there, I can't hear you."

Mercy suddenly remembered the other silent calls she had received. With thoughts of Robin stressing her out, and the fact that the calls had only come to her apartment's phone line, it had taken her awhile to remember. Now, she pursed her lips and listened intently. She fully expected the heavy breathing to start up at any moment. It never did.

Mercy hung up her phone, figuring it was just a bad connection, and returned to the living room. She collapsed onto the sofa, nervously flipping the cell around in her hands. It started to ring again. She looked at the display and saw that it was her mom's cell calling.

"Mom?" she answered.

"Hey Mercy, it's your dad," he replied. "Your mom is still with Tom and Emily."

Already Mercy was relieved. If the news was really bad, Mercy's mom would have wanted to tell her herself. Also, although her dad's voice sounded tired, it didn't carry the choked-up strain of bad news.

"Hi, Dad. So do the doctors know what's wrong, yet?"

"They're fairly certain it was an allergic reaction of some sort. They're running some kind of allergy panel on Robin right now. The current theory is that Emily ate something he's allergic to, and it got into him through her milk."

Mercy found herself nodding, even though her dad couldn't see her. "That doesn't sound too bad then."

"Still, they want to keep him overnight."

"Better safe than sorry when it comes to infants." Mercy remembered how fast everything moved in the ER whenever an infant came in. With their little, not fully-developed bodies, even the smallest thing could end terribly.

"There's a hotel across the street. Your mom wants to check into it so we can stay nearby. She's trying to convince Tom and Emily to spend the night there with us, but I don't think that's going to happen."

"No, probably not."

"Either way, we're not going to be home tonight."

"Is it okay if I stay here for the night?" She didn't feel up to driving home while a sizable chunk of her family was going to be spending most of the night in a hospital. Besides, her mother would love to see her when she got home. It would make both women feel better about the whole thing.

"Of course, but don't you have work tomorrow morning?"

"I'm starting a run of late shifts. I don't have to be into work until late in the afternoon."

"All right, then. Feel free to sleep in whatever room you'd like."

"Thanks, Dad."

"No problem, kiddo. We'll call again if anything changes."

"See you tomorrow."

"Bye, Mercy."

Both Mercy and her dad hung up.

The good news buoyed Mercy's spirits. Things could have been a lot worse than an allergy. A *lot* worse.

She called Kenny and told him everything that had happened with Robin, and that she'd be staying at her parents' house overnight. He said he was glad that Robin was okay, and that he'd try to be home early enough to see her before she went into work. He and the guys had booked the Monday off for a long weekend.

Still feeling good, Mercy finally had an appetite. She went back into the kitchen and took her plate out of the warming drawer. She ate at a little table in the corner of the kitchen rather than in the large dining room. Afterward, she wrapped up the other plates in tinfoil, found room for them in the fridge, and ate a small bowl of her mom's pudding.

The sun had set, but it wasn't yet late enough for Mercy to feel like going to bed. Still, she headed upstairs, intending to go through her sister's room to borrow a pair of pajamas. She'd be more comfortable sitting around in them than in her sundress.

Once on the stairs, which led up from the kitchen, the look of the house began to change. The steps were covered in a beige carpet, and as she ascended them, the wooden walls became a neutral, pale yellow-painted plaster. More of Mercy's mother's photography adorned the walls up the staircase, but the upper hallways were lined with family photos, mostly from Mercy and her siblings' younger years. Mercy navigated the hallway with ease, not bothering to turn on the overhead light. She found Faith's room and went in.

The room was painted pink, the carpet and ceiling blue, and it was cleaner than Mercy was used to seeing it. Since her little sister was living in residence while she was off learning, a few items were clearly gone, but major things like her dresser and bed were still present. The bright green sheets covering the bed blazed in the corner of Mercy's eye as she walked over to the multi-coloured dresser. Faith had always loved bright colours, even if they clashed terribly. At least while crossing the room, she didn't have to worry about getting tangled up in the clothes-amoeba that usually lived on the floor. Most of the dresser was empty, its overflowing contents temporarily moved out, but there were a few items left behind, including a white sleeping shirt and silky, navy blue pajama bottoms. After changing, Mercy made her way to her old room, which was now a guest room. It had changed a lot since she lived here. The dark brown carpet was changed to grey, the sunshine yellow walls were now a forest green with a palm leaf pattern imprinted in a lighter shade of green, and all her personal possessions were gone. The bed frame was still the same one, however, with new blankets that better matched the new colour scheme. Where her desk had once stood was now all her mother's sewing equipment and her dresser had been replaced by a squatter, longer set of drawers that held material and clothing scraps. Mercy draped her sundress over the back of the chair. She had carried her cell phone upstairs with her, and dropped it onto the sewing table. No matter what changed in her room, the view remained the same. Well, almost the same, a big tree had fallen over maybe half a dozen years back. After staring at the stump for a bit, remembering the times she had climbed that particular tree, Mercy decided to go downstairs and watch some TV.

While the living room was on one side of the house, a nearly identical room they called the TV room, sat at the opposite end. Both rooms had similar décor but the TV room had a massive flat-screen hanging off the wall instead of a fireplace. It also had many shelves containing a wide variety of films. Mercy's dad watched at least one movie a day, partly for his own enjoyment and partly as research for future projects. He watched every making-of featurette he could get his hands on. Mercy didn't really want to watch a movie though, and decided to find out what was on TV.

After flipping through a bunch of channels, Mercy finally settled on a sitcom. She didn't follow any TV shows regularly, but this was a good one where even a passerby like Mercy would find the jokes funny.

The house phone started ringing.

The display on the phone in the TV room wasn't functioning, but even if it had been, Mercy didn't look at it. She had forgotten to call

Mrs. Abram and now assumed that it was probably just her, asking for an update.

"Hello, Chalmers residence. This is Mercy speaking." Mercy found herself falling back into her old patterns. Her mother had insisted they all answer the phone a certain way when they were little.

"Hello, Mercy Chalmers."

The voice on the other end was not that of Mrs. Abram. It was smooth, and awful, and was the voice that had haunted her own home line the last few days.

Mercy didn't feel fear. She was tired of being afraid. This time she felt anger, bordering on fury. A long rant started up in her head. She wanted to yell and scream at this man, but she was just so angry that all she could manage to do was clench her teeth.

"How are you this evening, Mercy? Well? Are you enjoying yourself?"

Mercy didn't answer.

"Tell me, do you actually enjoy that piece of crap show you're watching? I find the blond bitch to be incredibly irritating."

Cold fear found its way into Mercy, moving her unexpected anger to one side. She rose to her feet, slowly.

"Please, don't bother getting up."

The man could see her. Mercy looked toward the nearest windows. None of the curtains were drawn and all she could see through them was an endless black void. She felt exposed in the middle of the room. There were several directions in which he could be, but Mercy had no idea. She relied on her nurse's training to keep her exterior calm while her heart raced within her chest.

"We need to have a talk, you and I, but not over the phone. That's too... impersonal, I think. See you soon."

The phone went completely dead, not even a dial tone replaced the cold voice. At nearly the same time, the cable went dead as well, the TV declaring that there was no signal. Mercy barely had enough time to read the message, however, as the power then went out, plunging her into the darkness that had been pressing in on the windows.

CHAPTER FOUR

MERCY REACTED A LOT faster than she expected she could. The moment the lights went out, she dropped the phone to the floor and dashed for the door. She nearly killed herself when her legs met a low footstool on the way, but she managed to keep her balance and keep going, although her shin now throbbed. The lock was still open from when she had entered earlier, so she threw it closed. The loud *snap* was a little comforting. Next she ran around the entire first floor: from TV room, to reading room, to kitchen, to dining room, to living room. In every room she checked that the window locks were engaged and pulled all the curtains shut. Her legs met furniture a few more times, but none were serious impacts as her night vision had already improved. Also while in the kitchen, Mercy locked the back door, propping one of the kitchen chairs against the doorknob for extra security.

Finishing her circuit back in the entrance hall, she stood as still as the stones beneath her feet. Her breathing came in short, rapid gasps, which she did her best to keep silent. Her eyes were wide as they finished adjusting to the gloom. The only lights in the house now came from a few flashlights plugged into the walls; the battery safety feature had turned them on when the power went out. There was one in the living room and one in the reading room, but Mercy didn't go to either. She knew the house well enough to navigate with minimal light and figured a flashlight would do nothing but give away her position. She was impressed by her own mind's reasoning and swift thoughts.

As she stood still, Mercy listened for any unusual sounds. There were none. Everything seemed normal. Just as she began to think that maybe she had overreacted, a bright light blasted in through the front windows. Mercy shielded her eyes and positioned herself against the front door, beneath the inset window. The light shone in over her head through that window, as well as through the heavy sidelights on either side of the door. Mercy trembled.

Slowly, she shifted sideways, allowing only one eye to look through the right sidelight. The light was blinding, but she was able to discern that a pair of high beams was causing it. Due to the bright lights, it was impossible to make out the vehicle casting them, or if anybody was near it.

Music blasted at the house from the vehicle. Some sort of country tune that Mercy didn't know rattled the windows lightly. She quickly ducked her head back behind the door, wondering if she had been seen.

Keeping her eyes on the front door, Mercy slowly walked backward in a crouch through the house. Perhaps she could sneak out through the back door and run to the Abrams'. The loud music almost made her miss the sound of the chair crashing to the floor in the kitchen. The back door had been opened!

Realizing the lights and the music must have been just a distraction, she ran back to the front door. The doorknob there was rattling. Mercy had assumed there was only one man, working alone. Now she knew there had to be two; there was just no way one man could run around the house in that small amount of time since the chair had crashed to the floor. There were at least two men.

Mercy headed back into the TV room, wondering what she should do. If there were two, there could easily be more. What if the whole house was surrounded?

The light from the flashlight in the reading room dimmed. Someone was passing between it and the TV room. Mercy went in the only direction left to her: her dad's office.

She opened the door across from the TV and dashed through it. Through a tiny crack as she pulled the door closed behind her, she saw a dark shape appear in the reading room's doorway and heard the front door's lock snap open. At least she was pretty sure she heard the lock snap open; it was hard to tell because of the music. Whoever these guys were, they seemed to know all about picking locks.

Once the office door was firmly shut behind her, Mercy was plunged into complete darkness. She stepped away from the door, her hands groping for familiar objects. In her mind, she pictured her dad's office. It was small, in the centre of the house, and under the stairs. There were no windows, as her dad didn't like the distraction of the outside world. To the left, toward the kitchen, the stairs sloped overhead. On the step backs hung photos of Mercy's dad with famous people he had met, and under them, were lock boxes containing the final versions of film scripts, personal records, and even the coveted Oscar statue. To the right, the wall was hung with movie posters from the films he had written. On the back wall was a large array of shelves, which held those same movies, the rolled-up posters he didn't want to hang, and stacks of old script drafts. In the middle of all of this was a large desk, holding a laptop, a few external hard drives, a printer, a fax machine, a modem, a router, and a telephone.

The desk is what Mercy sought, trying to get her bearings. She recalled it being waist high, but it was actually lower. Her hands passed right over it, allowing her thighs to slam painfully into the edge. Her natural reaction was to suck in a sharp breath, but she smothered the impulse, even clamping a hand over her mouth.

She wondered if the men had heard her bump into the desk. There was no time to think about that now. Mercy worked her way around the desk, locating the wheeled chair behind it. She was very careful not to move the chair, as the wheels would rattle along the hardwood flooring.

Her hands fluttered along the desk until they found the laptop. She pulled open the lid and bathed the room in light from the screen. Thank God for a battery charge. Her dad had left the laptop on and

Mercy knew the password to get into it. A picture of her and her siblings greeted her as the background of the desktop. The smiling faces seemed so surreal in the dark with her heart beating out a rhythm of terror. Several windows had popped up to inform her that the hard drives and printer were disconnected—due to the power outage they were all powered off—but she ignored them. Pulling up the connection window, she searched for a signal. With the cable out, the Internet was down as well. There were no signals reaching the computer. If only her dad had bought a big battery back-up for the hard drives like Kenny had suggested! Then she could have plugged the modem and router into it and been good to go. At least in her mind, it would work that way, but Mercy actually knew very little about how the Internet functioned. Either way, thinking about what she didn't have did her no good.

Just in case, Mercy picked up the phone off the desk and held it to her ear. Nothing—no dial tone. She put the phone back. If she could get upstairs, she could reach her cell phone. It had been so stupid of her to leave it up in the guestroom after she had changed!

Mercy muted the laptop and unplugged it from the docking station. She lifted the computer up and began to walk around the room, praying that a signal would get through to her somewhere. She walked to every corner, crouched under the steps, held the laptop as close to the ceiling as possible, but nothing. There were no signals anywhere.

Frustrated and scared, Mercy closed the laptop and plunged the world back into darkness. But it wasn't completely dark. A light shone under the crack at the bottom of the door. The intruders were coming toward it!

Mercy had hoped that maybe they wouldn't check the office, that somehow they would miss it, or think it was a tiny closet. No such luck.

Without thought, Mercy pressed the button lock on the door. She backed away quickly, scrambling around the desk to the other side, putting the laptop down on it as she passed. Her hands began searching blindly along the shelves.

The doorknob rattled behind her.

Mercy started searching more frantically. Where was it? She bumped lightly into the desk chair as she searched. It rolled across the floor with a clatter.

Whoever was outside rattled the doorknob harder. He then slammed a fist against the wood.

"I know you're in there, my little Mercy," a voice called through the door. It was the voice from the telephone.

Mercy ignored it. She focused on her search.

The door was slammed with something heavy, probably a shoulder.

Mercy failed to suppress the squeak that escaped her. Her hands continued fumbling along the shelves, knocking things over now. Papers scattered all over the floor, fluttering against her legs and feet.

Wham!

Where was it?

Wham!

It was here somewhere.

Wham! Crack!

There's no time, where the bloody hell is it?

CRACK!

CHAPTER FIVE

Light from a flashlight pierced through the door where it met the jamb. The door wouldn't hold out much longer. Frankly, Mercy was surprised it had lasted this long.

There!

With the small beam of light, Mercy was able to spot what she had been searching for: a certain knot of wood. She slammed her fingers into it, bending them back painfully with the effort. The knot clicked in and part of the shelves swung outward into the living room.

The office door flung open with a crash, not surviving the last blow.

Without thinking, Mercy grabbed one of the DVDs and hurled it at the door. She missed the man about to enter, but the sudden projectile caused him to back away, his flashlight swinging upward. With the brief moment of darkness, Mercy fled into the living room.

She would have loved to close the door behind her, confuse the intruders, but there was no time. With the flashlight in the living room outlet still on and the high beams shining brightly through the front windows, Mercy was able to fly through the room, lithely avoiding the furniture. Though she flew through the dining room equally fast, she paused as she reached the kitchen, but only briefly. She felt she had to make sure nobody was in it. Peering around the entrance jamb, she saw that the kitchen was vacant. The back door hung wide open, the chair lying on the floor nearby.

Mercy was about to flee through the open door, but as she neared it, she saw a light outside. Either there was a third man, or one of the two had gone back out while Mercy had been screwing around with the laptop.

A light shone into the dining room from the living room. The intruder might be trying to decide which way Mercy had gone upon leaving the office, but she couldn't take the chance she'd have that extra time. She had to assume that the man was coming for her.

Mercy climbed up the stairs as fast as she dared. Although the carpet would help to muffle her footsteps, storming her way up the steps would undoubtedly cause a hell of a racket. As she climbed, she chastised herself for not grabbing a knife from the kitchen. When she reached the top step, Mercy glanced down, thinking that maybe she could still rush down and snatch one. A spear of light from a flashlight shining into the kitchen dashed her hopes.

At the top of the stairs, the first door was the bathroom. She bypassed it and hurried down the hall to the left. On the way to the guestroom, Mercy went past her sister's room. As she did, she grabbed the door handle and shut the door. With luck, it would slow down the intruder, as he'd need to check that room first. The next door was that of the guestroom, her former bedroom. She ducked in through the doorway and closed the door behind her, pushing in the button lock. A feeble defense.

Pausing for a moment, Mercy's heart continued hammering away in her chest. She hadn't really had any time to breathe or think. Her ear was pressed to the door, listening for any sounds. Realizing she wasn't likely to hear anything over the blasting country music, she pulled away. She needed to call the cops.

On the desk, her cell phone sat as a beacon of hope. She rushed over and scooped it up in her hands. She flipped open the phone.

There was nothing!

Panicked, Mercy jammed her thumb down on the power button. The cell phone wouldn't turn on. She absurdly thought that the intruders had somehow cut the power to her cell when they had the rest of the house. Of course that was impossible. She then had the idea that they had snuck up the stairs before Mercy, found her phone, and yanked the battery out. After pulling off the back, she quickly realized that that was an equally absurd idea.

The battery was dead, that was all. She had left her phone on overnight when she had slept with it on her nightstand, in case she had gotten scared while trying to sleep. That combined with all the phone calls made over the past two days equaled one flat battery.

Her lifeline was dead.

Mercy slowly dropped to the floor, sitting on her haunches. She gripped the phone tightly in her hands, willing it to spring back to life. Silent tears slipped down her cheeks. What was she going to do? She had no way to call for help. She was completely alone.

No, she wasn't going to just give up. That wasn't an acceptable option. She'd find a way to get out of the house, to get to someone with a working phone.

Mercy didn't have any pockets in the clothes that she was wearing, and so she had no way to bring the cell with her. Despite the fact that it was dead, she had to will her hand to open and put the phone down. Leaving it behind was difficult.

A creak, just loud enough to hear over the music, sounded from out in the hall. The intruder was near Faith's room. Mercy got back up on her feet. Turning to her mother's sewing supplies, she grabbed a pair of scissors. They wouldn't be the most effective weapon, but at least they were something. She hurried to the window and looked out.

The window at the back of the house overlooked the roof above the rear porch. Mercy debated it for a second, but she could still see the man with the flashlight out there. The beam was pointed at the house, sweeping back and forth. Fearing that she could be seen in the window, Mercy quickly slunk away. She checked the window at the side of the house, but below it was a sheer two-storey drop. There was a chance she would break a leg, or at least badly sprain an ankle. Mercy didn't have a lot going for her, but not being injured was one thing she did have. Besides, the movement might draw the attention of the man out back.

Left with only one option, Mercy went to the closet. The doorknob to the hall started to rattle.

"Haven't we already gone through this?" a voice called through the door, somewhat irritated.

The man started slamming his shoulder into it again. It wasn't likely to hold out as long as the office door had.

Mercy disappeared into the closet as he was speaking. She shut the door behind her, cloaking herself in darkness again. This time, she was better aware of the location of the secret passage; this had been her bedroom after all.

She knelt down in the cramped space and grabbed a vent near the floor. She pulled on the vent, separating it and a small section of wall. The space behind was large enough for a child, and, if squeezed, a thin adult. The bedroom door burst open with a crash. Clutching her scissors, Mercy wormed her way inside, head first, her elbows and knees scraping along the interior.

The closet door was ripped open behind her.

"Oi!" the man cried just as Mercy's feet slid into the space. He dropped to his stomach and reached in after her.

Mercy screamed and started kicking as best she could, her knees hitting the sides of the passage. Several times she felt the man's hands, covered in soft leather gloves, brush against her bare feet. She wormed farther into the space, using her kicks as leverage, until her hands hit a second vent. She slammed into the vent, popping it out with a piece of wall just like in her own closet.

Grabbing the edges of the space, Mercy was able to pull herself into her sister's closet. Behind her, the man growled in anger. He was trying to follow after her, but he was too big. He couldn't fit through the small space. The passage had been there when Mercy's grandparents got the place, and now, she silently thanked her dad for preserving it when he redid the rooms.

As Mercy sprang to her feet, she hit her shoulder on a rack in her sister's closet, a bolt pain punching through it. The man was already backing out of the hidden crawl space, probably realizing where Mercy had gone.

Lacking time, Mercy ignored her shoulder and spilled out into the brightly coloured room. She could hear the man running to the door of her room with a few long strides. Realizing she had no other choice, Mercy bolted for the window at the front of the house. She threw up the sash as the footsteps pounded toward the door. Scrambling outside onto the shingles above the porch, the grit scraped her palms.

"She's on the roof!" Mercy heard a second man's voice call out over the music. She glanced down as she got to her feet, pebbles sticking to her soles.

Standing above the high beams, Mercy was finally able to get a look at the vehicle. It was a huge, shiny, new-looking pickup truck. A man sat on the hood, his feet dangling in front of the grill. He wore a rubber cat mask over the top half of his face and a wide, toothy grin on the bottom. A wisp of smoke rose from the cigarette he held in one hand, while the other held a shotgun across his lap.

Mercy ran along the roof. She made it to the bathroom window and tugged it open, just as her pursuer began to climb out of Faith's room. The man on the truck giggled—a high and piercing sound.

"Shut that fucking music off!" the man after Mercy bellowed. She was already in the bathroom by the time he shouted it.

After running the few steps needed to cross the white tiled bathroom, Mercy entered the hallway again. She wanted to run back downstairs, but after reaching the first step, she put on the brakes.

Another man, this one wearing the upper half of a rubber rabbit mask, appeared at the bottom. He seemed just as surprised to see Mercy as she was to see him, and they both stopped, momentarily stunned.

The moment was broken when the man following Mercy crashed onto the bathroom floor having struggled in through the window.

Mercy spun to one side, heading for her brother's room.

"Hey!" rabbit mask called after her.

Tom's former room didn't have the same tunnel as hers. Even if it did, escaping through it was unlikely to work a second time. While Mercy's room had been turned into a sewing room, her brother's was the exercise room. After engaging the lock, she dragged the heavy weights over to the door and butted them up against it.

"She went that way!" It was rabbit mask's voice, probably directing the man following her.

A moment later, a heavy shoulder was slammed into the door.

"Get your fine ass out here!" the man shouted. "And you, tell that ass-wipe to turn off that goddamn music. I can't hear myself think."

Mercy wasn't sure if she wanted the music to stop. Although it covered the sounds of the men's movements, it had also covered her own. She decided to make the most of it while it was still on.

In the corner of this room's ceiling was a panel that led up into the attic space. Mercy had only been in the attic a handful of times, but it was the only way out of the room. Other than going out on the porch roof again, that was, but she figured that would be pointless, as the man with the shotgun would call out her position again. The sight of the shotgun terrified her. Whatever these men wanted, they were serious about getting it.

Beneath the plywood panel was a treadmill. Mercy climbed up and balanced upon the handles and control bar. She threw her shoulder into the plywood. It didn't budge; it was stuck. Mercy started throwing her shoulder repeatedly into it, putting her whole body into it. One side started to give first. Then the whole thing popped loose. After that, Mercy just had to lift the panel up with her hands, and pull herself through. It was dark in the attic, but not pitch-black: a small skylight brought in a dim glow.

The music outside finally stopped.

"What are you doing?" a voice Mercy hadn't heard before called out. She assumed it was cat mask's voice.

"Going in through the window, what does it look like?" responded the man's voice from eerily close by.

Mercy slid the panel back into place just as the window was opened. Very slowly, she moved a nearby box to rest on top of the plywood square. It wasn't heavy, but she couldn't risk trying to move anything else. She wasn't even aware what else was around her. Mercy listened intently, her ear pressed to where the panel met the ceiling. The man searched the room, ripping open the closet and kicking at vents. A light appeared around the edges of the panel as he shone his flashlight at it. The light then disappeared.

"She's in the attic!" the man called out through the window. "You, get back up here and watch for when she pops out someplace else. I'm going to flush her out."

Mercy crawled away from the panel. She could just make out the sounds of the man moving the weights away from the door, and used that distraction to crawl farther away.

She didn't know the layout of the attic.

As she crawled along, she bumped into all sorts of objects. The skylight provided barely enough light to highlight the edges of the largest items. Mercy didn't know where to go. The panel in her brother's old room was the only way into the attic that she knew of. She could try hiding amongst the old furniture and boxes of memorabilia, but she doubted she could succeed at that for very long. The man had a flashlight. He'd be able to navigate the warren of junk a lot easier than Mercy could. If Mercy did try to hide, she wouldn't even know how good her hiding space was until she was or wasn't found.

Her head bumped into the low ceiling. Mercy had crawled too far to one side, where the roof sloped down to the walls. Gritting her teeth from the goose egg that must be forming, she turned and made her way back toward a more central area of the attic. She found herself under the skylight.

Whump.

The man was trying to open the panel, the box on top jumping from the impact. Mercy looked up, pleading with God. Instead, she saw the skylight's latch. She could open it.

Moving fast, Mercy climbed onto a small dresser beneath the window. It wobbled dangerously beneath her feet, the boxes on top trembling alongside her. She stood and tugged at the window latch, balancing precariously. The latch was stiff, like the panel had been.

Whump.

The latch finally turned. She pushed the window open, nearly tumbling over in the process. She just managed to grab hold of the window frame to keep from falling over. She pulled herself up and through the opening.

As she closed the skylight behind her, there was a loud crash as the box on top of the panel was finally knocked over. Mercy couldn't help but wonder if anything precious to her mother was in that box.

The man below would be beginning his search. There was no telling when he'd think to check out the skylight, and there was no doubt in Mercy's mind that he would eventually. He didn't know there wasn't another way back into the house, however, and after the secret passages, it seemed likely he'd think there was.

Mercy figured she had some time. She searched around herself, the only light coming from the high beams below and the stars above; it was a moonless night. There was nothing but shingles and the brick chimney rising up along one side, and neither of those would do her any good.

As Mercy lay on the roof, the cool night air caressing her bumps and scrapes, she realized she had just traded a place she could hide in for one in which she couldn't.

CHAPTER SIX

IF A SECOND STORY window was too high for Mercy to risk dropping from, then the roof was totally out of the question. She inched back from the edge, grateful for the gentle slope. Had the house been built with a steeper peak, she probably would have toppled over the edge by now.

She was running out of time. Every second spent on the roof brought her another second closer to when the man would check out the skylight. She had already wasted so much time just exploring the roof, moving at a snail's pace so as not to give away her position. She wished the music was back on.

The man in the cat mask was still sitting on the pickup truck's hood. He was whistling. Mercy couldn't identify the tune, as he was very off-key and couldn't carry any sort of tempo.

Why were these men doing this? Mercy couldn't think of a single reason why a group of men would terrorize her this way. Her mind jumped to the obvious conclusions of rape and murder. But was it just that? Why the phone calls first? Maybe it was just a group of dumb, bored, adolescents who wanted to get a rise out of a stranger, and when she came up here and they found her alone, they took it too far. Although that was just it: this had already gone too far.

Whoever these guys were, they knew how to pick locks, cut the power, and cut the phone lines. The shotgun was still the most frightening aspect. Did the others have guns too?

They were chasing her through the house, so it couldn't be just a robbery. And again, the phone calls. Also, they had taken a big risk.

They didn't know that Mercy's cell phone had a dead battery. For all they knew, she had already called the cops.

And yet, here they were, still hunting for her. They were either very stupid, or, somehow, they knew she hadn't called the police. But how could they know that?

Mercy's thoughts were cut off as she peered over the edge again and spotted her way off the roof. It was going to be very risky, but Mercy thought it would be safer than trying to confront her pursuer with nothing better than a pair of scissors.

Very slowly, she inched her way along toward the corner where the eavestrough met the downspout. Mercy snaked a hand under the eaves and grabbed the spout. She tugged on it, testing its durability. The downspout was solidly bolted to the wall and tightly connected to the eaves. It was impossible to tell if it could hold her weight, but Mercy had to try. As she eased her shoulders to the edge, her head hanging out into space, she realized that she would need both her hands to do this. There was no way to keep hold of the scissors. Without any other choice, Mercy tucked the scissors into the waistband of the pajama pants she wore, so that they rested against the small of her back. They didn't feel very secure there, but she couldn't of anything else to do with them.

A clattering of boxes was heard coming through the roof beneath her. It was impossible to tell where the sound had come from precisely, but Mercy felt certain it was the boxes on the dresser from beneath the window. The man was coming.

Mercy scooted closer to the edge. The more she thought about it, the worse this idea became. Twisting her arm at an awkward angle, she wrapped it over the section of downspout that slanted from the eaves to the wall of the house. At that precarious angle, with a fair amount of her upper torso past the eaves, she suddenly decided that this was an extremely terrible idea. There was no way she wasn't going to get hurt. Maybe she should hurry back to the window and stab the man with the scissors as he came out.

It was too late to change her mind. Her body shifted only a tiny bit, but it was enough to overbalance her. The slide started slowly at first, and Mercy's mind slowed it down even further. She was aware of what was happening but there was nothing she could do about it. The roof ejected her over its edge.

Reacting instinctively, her hand tightened its grip on the downspout. She was swung sideways as she fell and her other hand quickly reached up and latched onto the spout as well. The momentum threatened to rip her off completely, but she clung on like a bird in a storm. The scissors couldn't hold on in the waistband of her pants. She felt them slip free and slide all the way down her leg. Mercy didn't watch them fall to the ground so far below, but she heard them hit. The eaves groaned with her weight, the downspout threatening to pop free at any moment. Slowly, one hand at a time, she moved closer to the wall, where the strain was put on the much more stable brackets.

The skylight in the roof was opened. Mercy listened as the man climbed out and started to look around. Her arms were screaming from the strain of hanging there and her hands cramped, but she didn't dare move. Movement could result in the downspout creaking, which the man would likely hear, and then all would be for naught.

The heavy footsteps came toward her position. Mercy bit her lower lip, sweat popping out in beads upon her forehead. It felt like her shoulders were going to rip out of their sockets at any moment. The footsteps stopped just above her head. She imagined the man was looking over the edge, seeing if she was somewhere down below. If he leaned out far enough, he would surely spot her dangling feet.

The footsteps retreated, heading toward the roof's opposite corner. Once they crossed over the peak, Mercy had to risk moving. If she didn't, her hands would surely give out.

Stretching her leg to one side, she reached for the windowsill to her parents' bedroom. Her toes kept brushing the edge, but she couldn't get a grip. With one last effort, she threw her weight to the side and managed to get her foot on the sill. The downspout creaked ominously. For a moment, she stayed still, her hands wrapped around the downspout and her body stretched awkwardly to one side, with only one foot planted. The spout held and the footsteps didn't return her way.

By shifting her balance and sliding her foot over, Mercy was able to get her other foot up and onto the sill. Her body was now being pulled between her hands on the downspout, and her feet upon the sill. Terrifying herself, she let go with one hand and shot it toward the window with lightning speed. She grabbed hold of the window frame before losing her balance and pressed her fingers into the wood. She just had to let go with her other hand now, although her body was still hanging over air.

Mercy took a deep breath and released. Her handhold on the window frame was not as secure as she thought. Without her other arm supporting her body, her fingers started to slip. She grabbed at the house's wooden siding with her free hand, managing to balance herself but smacking the wall in the process. She quickly scrambled to get all of her weight onto the sill. She was so glad that her father had made it as wide as he had. Would have been nice if it were even wider, but still.

Hunched over to fit beneath the eaves, Mercy looked in through the glass. As she peered through a gap in the curtains, she saw the rabbit-masked man walk into the room. He must have heard her when she hit the side of the house.

Mercy crunched herself up against the window, trying to keep her body behind the curtains and out of sight. Although she knew it was dangerous to do so, part of her couldn't resist peering through the space between the curtains with one eye.

Rabbit mask walked slowly through the room, treading lightly. The mask was creepy. It made Mercy think of a game that Kenny would sometimes play. It was some sort of horror game so Mercy never hung around in the room when he played it, but she remembered the enemies wore half-masks like this man. The rabbit-masked man was thin beneath his baggy clothes; Mercy could tell at least that much about him. When he turned to look inside a massive wardrobe across the room from her, she could see the dirty white elastic of the mask cutting through his lank, stringy hair. It looked like it hadn't been washed in awhile and stuck up in places.

After he checked out the wardrobe, he went over to the door that led into the small ensuite bathroom. The beam of his flashlight landed upon the dark tile and bright fixtures. He even searched behind the shower curtain. Back in the bedroom, he checked under the king-sized bed, checked in the closet, and poked around in the large drawers of Mercy's mother's dresser. Mercy's mom would be so embarrassed and angry to learn that a strange man had pawed through her undergarments.

He then walked up to the window along the back wall, the one that led out onto the roof of the back porch. Rabbit mask threw aside the curtains and peered out. He lifted up the sash and poked out his head, checking to see if Mercy was hiding out there. He then turned to the curtains that were hiding Mercy from view, and she pulled her head out of sight.

Her legs trembled. When the man threw back the curtains, and he would, she would be in plain sight. There was no way to hide herself on the sill without the curtains. Briefly, she considered trying to get back to the downspout, but that would be suicide. She doubted she'd be able to get back to it, and even if she could, she was bound to make some noise and alert the rabbit-masked man to her position. Or the downspout would finally give in and snap loose of the eaves, dumping Mercy off to fall to the ground below.

She waited and waited, but the curtains weren't drawn back. With curiosity eating away at her, Mercy dared to peer in again. Rabbit mask's back was to her. He was walking stealthily toward the door, away from her, his flashlight turned off. Something else must have drawn his attention. While she watched, he pulled up the side of his large, black hoody and revealed a pistol in a holster on his belt. Mercy's mouth went dry as he placed a hand on the butt of the gun.

A man appeared in the doorway and both of them startled, the rabbit-masked man pulling out his gun but not aiming it.

"Jesus Christ," the man who entered grumbled. His voice was that of the one who had been pursuing Mercy. He was a large man, much broader in the shoulders, and a few inches taller than rabbit mask. His arms filled out his own black, hooded sweatshirt. On his face was a half mask like the others, but his was a rat.

Rabbit mask holstered his pistol again. "I thought I heard a noise."

"Find anything?"

"Does it look like I found anything?"

"Go outside and see if she slipped away somehow. I'll start checking over this whole damn house, tearing it apart board by board if I have to."

Rabbit mask nodded, his rubber ears bobbling. He left the room. When the rat-masked man started to scan the bedroom, Mercy quickly pulled herself behind the curtain. She waited a full minute before peering back into the room again. It was now empty.

Contorting herself to reach down, Mercy was able to grab the bottom of the window. She very carefully pulled it open, going slowly to reduce noise and to maintain balance. She was so glad that she hadn't locked the upstairs windows after she had gone around locking the downstairs ones.

Once Mercy slipped inside, she spent a few precious seconds just lying on her parents' plush carpet. She wasn't done yet, though; she had to secure the room.

Back on her feet, Mercy tiptoed over to the doorway. She slowly poked her head around the jamb and into the hallway. It was empty. She couldn't tell where either man was in the house. Risking that the rat could've been right around the corner, or in her brother's room next door, she shut the door. She made sure to hold the handle down until the latch had passed the jamb, reducing the sound of the click.

With the door closed and locked, Mercy went to her mother's low dresser. She took off everything that sat on top of it, and placed it all carefully on the floor. Then, with more effort than she expected it to take, she slid the dresser over the carpet to rest in front of the door. The entire time there was that slight grinding sound of a heavy object sliding over carpet, but Mercy hoped she had moved it at a slow and steady enough pace for no one else to have heard.

Mercy finally had a moment to breathe. She lay down on top of her parents' large bed, the cushy comforter giving way beneath her and partly enveloping her like soft foam. She was so tired. All her muscles ached and everywhere there were scratches and bruises. Where she had hit her thigh on her dad's desk throbbed in time with her heartbeat, as did the lump on her head from the attic, and her shoulder from her sister's closet.

She knew she couldn't just keep lying there. She finally had time to think, and so she needed to come up with a plan. Struggling against her sore body, Mercy rose back up and sat with her legs dangling over the edge of the bed. They would find her eventually. All the men had to do was look down the hall toward the master bedroom and they would see that the door was closed when they had left it open.

Wracking her exhausted brain, Mercy thought about how to escape.

CHAPTER SEVEN

SHE WANTED TO SLEEP. Mercy would have liked nothing better than to curl up under the covers, close her eyes, and drift off into a dreamless slumber.

The men wouldn't let her do that though. These men were relentless. They had guns. Whatever it was they wanted from Mercy, they intended to get it.

Mercy couldn't think of a single reason why someone would be after her. But here she was, with not one, but three men forcing her to become a prisoner in her parents' house. And there could be more. She still wasn't sure if there was someone else out there, skulking around in the dark.

Mercy spied out the window, watching as the rabbit mask passed beneath her. He strolled along, flashlight in hand. If she were a random person who drove by at that exact moment, she would assume he was just out bringing in some firewood, or maybe going to turn on the generator because the power was out. But no one was going to drive by and think that. No one was going to drive by at all.

The sheep had left the field, had wandered off over the hills. Somewhere beyond those hills was the Abrams' place. They were the closest people for miles around. If Mercy could get to them, she could get help. It was getting to them that was the problem.

Mercy thought back to her childhood and teenaged years, when she had still lived in this house. She thought back to all the construction that had occurred: the torn-up walls, the plastic sheeting, the planning at the kitchen table. Her father had a fondness for the secret passages.

Although the girls had been a bit old at the time for the secret tunnel, he had chosen to keep it there, and just make it nicer. Mercy and Faith had been sneaking between each other's rooms their entire lives. It turned out that even as teenagers they would use the tunnel, mostly to steal clothes from closets, but sometimes when they just wanted to talk through the night about things. Despite the five-year age gap, the sisters were very close.

All these flooding memories were nice, but they weren't helping Mercy. The real question was, were there any passages and secret ways that could help her right now?

There was a hidden dumbwaiter in the kitchen, but that only led to the basement. The basement wasn't used much. It was mostly a workshop and storage for tools. Mercy would have loved to have her dad's big hedge clippers right about now. Those would be a lot better than the dinky scissors she had been carrying. Also in the basement was a wine rack and the laundry machines.

The laundry...

Mercy got up and hurried over to her parents' closet. She pulled open the door and dropped to her knees. There, in the closet floor, was a little hinged panel. She pulled back the bolt and flipped up the hatch. It revealed a laundry chute that went straight down into the basement. Mercy remembered all the times she had sat in the living room and could hear her mother singing as she cleaned the bedroom. Her voice would carry down the chute and in through the walls between the living and dining rooms.

As she looked down, she saw a light at the bottom moving about. It was probably the rat, searching for her in the basement, his flashlight moving this way and that. It made her realize that the basement was a long way down. Perhaps it wasn't the means of escape she had been searching for.

There was always the roof over the back porch. She could run along it and get to her old room just as she had moved across the front porch's roof. But where would that get her? Once there, what then? She couldn't keep running in circles.

Maybe there was something in her parents' bedroom that she could use.

Mercy started searching. She went through the closet, the wardrobe, the dresser, and the bathroom. The most useful thing she found was a nail file, and she could think of no use for it other than as a crude weapon. She even went up to the bed and starting ripping the sheets and blankets off of it. For a moment, Mercy considered shoving the mattress out of the window and then jumping after it. The mattress would never fit through the frame of course, and it was so big, she would barely be able to push it onto the floor by herself.

She wished Kenny was with her. He would know what to do. Actually, he had a gun and could probably just shoot the sons of bitches. Or, better yet, call in a fucking SWAT team on his cell phone. Even having her dog, Roofus, with her would have been a lot better than being so completely alone. Roofus wasn't exactly the bravest and boldest of dogs, but just having some company would have made Mercy feel a bit better, a bit less like a tightened piano wire.

Maybe they would give up. Maybe the men would stop looking for her before they discovered that she was upstairs.

If Mercy hadn't been so alone, she would have been sorely tempted to believe that. As it was, she had only herself to rely upon. She couldn't just hope for the best. Her father had taught her that things don't always work out the way you hoped, that you had to fight for what you wanted. Right now, Mercy was pretty sure she was fighting for her very life. She couldn't give in to hopeless temptation. She needed to think. She needed to stop trembling.

Mercy looked around the bedroom again. Maybe she could hide in the wardrobe. One of the men was sure to check it out, but perhaps she could surprise him. Maybe even manage to stab him with the nail file. If she could do that, she could probably run past him, get out of the room, run down the stairs, and flee out the back door. There were a lot of problems with that plan.

"Oh, Mercy? I know you're in there."

Mercy's blood turned to ice. The rat was right outside the bedroom door. When had he come back upstairs?

"Why don't you make this easy and come on out?" he said. His voice dripped with intent. If Mercy opened that door, she couldn't even begin to imagine what would happen to her.

She stood as still as a frog in the presence of a heron. And like that frog, she needed to find a quick get-away.

The handle jiggled, and then the now familiar hammering started. Every hit went to the core of her being.

The porch roof. She was going to jump off the porch roof. Screw the fact that her brother had broken his leg doing the exact same thing, she had no other choice.

"Go around," the rat said to someone out there with him. "Make sure she doesn't cross the roof again. Go in through the window."

Footsteps hurried down the hall, toward Mercy's former bedroom.

Fuck. She couldn't risk the porch now.

There was no time. She ran to the bed. Calling up a strength she had never known, she tilted the massive mattress up and out of the bed frame. On its side, she continued pushing and shoving it around until it rested against the window that led to the porch roof. It wouldn't hold back the man for long, but it would give her a few more precious seconds.

Mercy grabbed all the clothing, bed sheets, and towels that she could. She began stuffing them all down the laundry chute. They fell to the basement floor far below. She didn't stop shoving until everything was in there, even throwing down her mother's good dress, the one she had worn to the Academy Awards. A small clog formed in the chute; something that Mercy's mother hated but that Mercy was grateful for.

"The fuck?" a muffled voice said from the other side of the mattress. It began to wiggle as the man started pushing on it from outside.

Mercy threw on one of her dad's sweatshirts and grabbed her mom's weekend socks. The socks were very wooly and had rubber dots stuck to the bottoms for grip. Mercy pulled the socks onto her feet the moment she dropped to the floor next to the closet. Without hesitation, she slid her feet into the chute. They were promptly followed by her legs, her torso, her arms, and her head.

Going down the chute was faster and noisier than Mercy would have liked. She pressed her forearms and feet into the sides as best she could, but that only somewhat slowed her down. When she hit the clog, it slowed her down a bit more, but it became instantly unjammed, the bundle of cloth falling away beneath her. Before she knew it, her legs were in space, and then so was the rest of her. She hit the pile of clothes and sheets and towels and let her legs crumple under her, rolling to one side. Pins and needles shot up to her hips, and her hands hit the hard floor with a smack. Her head bumped into the floor after that, causing her to bite her lower lip.

Lying there, Mercy assessed herself. Her limbs still worked, and she didn't think she had broken or sprained anything. Her lip was bleeding and likely to start swelling soon, but that didn't matter. She could still move, that was what mattered.

Descending the laundry chute had been accompanied by a great deal of rattling. Even with the rat trying to hammer his way through the door, there was no way they wouldn't have heard that.

Mercy sprang to her feet, her legs protesting. She booted it to the stairs and began leaping up two steps at a time. As she reached the top, she heard thunderous footfalls from upstairs making their way to the top of the staircase.

The kitchen door was still open. Mercy ran to it, grabbing the knife block off the counter as she passed by. She burst out into the nighttime air, footsteps running along the porch's roof above her. She turned to run toward the sheep field.

Cat mask was there.

Mercy had naturally assumed that cat mask was still sitting on the truck's hood. Without thinking, she threw the knife block with all her might, then turned and ran in the opposite direction. She didn't even bother to glance back to see if she had hit her target.

Mercy ran for the woods, her socks slapping across the dewy grass.

As she reached the tree line, the bark from a tree next to her exploded. A sound like a big firework going off behind her told her that she had been shot at. She didn't feel like she had been hit though, so she kept on running.

Weaving through the trees, leaping over bushes, and bulling her way through low branches, Mercy entered the woods.

CHAPTER EIGHT

Mercy's breathing came in ragged gasps. Her lungs burned within her chest. Her feet were terribly sore, the socks doing little to protect them. She was quite sure she was bleeding from a few places now, not just her lip. The shirt and pajama pants were doing an all right job of protecting the skin on her arms and legs, but there was little she could do for her face. Without adequate lighting, there were branches she couldn't see until they struck her. A red welt on her cheek pulsed with pain from the last branch she had met.

She couldn't keep running. Without having any other choice, Mercy finally collapsed into the carpet of dead leaves. The greenery had only just begun to return to the woods, and most things were still dark and skeletal. The coniferous trees were still as bushy as ever, however, so Mercy crawled her way over to one and pressed herself up against it. Sap instantly attached itself to her fingers, but she hardly noticed.

It was hard to hear anything over the pounding of her heart and the rushing of air passing in and out of her lungs. She tried to get her breathing under control. Swallowing a few times, Mercy did everything she could to calm herself. Not an easy task when her mind was racing.

Eventually, she was able to hear another sound: heavy boots on dead leaves. Mercy listened closely, trying to pin-point the source before moving. It wasn't close, but it wasn't far off either. She peered around the base of the pine tree.

The beam of a flashlight weaved and bobbed along, causing sharp shadows to jump from the bones of the bushes and trees it fell upon.

Mercy couldn't identify which man it was from her hiding spot. He staggered a bit, probably as winded as she felt, except his feet wouldn't be as raw. As she watched, he slowed his pace even further. Perhaps he was using his own ears and had realized that Mercy's frantic crashing through the woods had ceased.

She looked around and located the trail she'd made. Even without being trained to track things, Mercy could see clearly that something had recently plowed through the area. She had left behind a wake of destruction: broken branches, trampled bushes and ferns, even foot prints in the exposed dirt. It wouldn't take long for the man with the flashlight to find her trail, which would lead him right to her.

Although every cell inside her wanted to stay put and hunker down, like when she'd paused on her parents' bed, she needed to move. She needed to take action.

Mercy tried to figure out where she was in the woods. She had spent a lot of time running through the trees as a child, but now everything seemed so foreign. She wasn't used to navigating the forest at night, and nature had had a way of changing things since she was a little girl. If only she had paid more attention while running she might know where she was, but she hadn't been able to when the latest dump of adrenaline had been coursing through her.

"If 'ifs' and 'buts' were candies and nuts, then no one would ever go hungry."

Mercy nearly slapped herself in the face when she realized she had spoken out loud. Although it was barely a whisper, she was afraid that any noise might give away her position. She glanced back toward the beam of light and noted that it hadn't changed its search pattern. For now she was okay.

Looking around the woods again, Mercy decided that it didn't matter where she was. All that mattered was not being found by the men in masks. She just had to pick a direction, move away from them, hide, and wait until they left. There was no way they could possibly search the entire woods for her.

Spotting a shallow gully, Mercy left the cover of the pine tree and headed toward it. The gully would provide her with protection while also leading away from the roving flashlight. It would only be a matter of seconds now before the man found her trail.

While Mercy walked, she watched her footing. It was slower going, but she avoided the dry sticks and leaves to the best of her ability. She minimized the amount of noise she made and the trail left behind her. By the time she reached the end of the gully, she could look back and no longer see the beam of light. Of course, natural rises in the land could have simply blocked it.

Mercy studied the land some more, since it would have changed the least over the years. She still didn't see anything she recognized. It was possible that she was in a section of the woods she didn't know. When walking, she usually didn't go in too deeply, and on four-wheelers and dirt bikes she had always stuck to the paths. If she could find one of those paths, then she'd know where she was, but for now, she just had to keep going and hope for the best.

Trees, bushes, rocks, trees, rocks, bushes, rocks, trees; the view never really changed.

After awhile, Mercy had to stop again. Her feet were killing her. She found a large flat rock and sat on top of it, drawing up her knees. The socks she had grabbed were once white; they weren't white any longer. Dirt had ground its way into every fiber. Quite a few of the rubber dots had been torn off. The only parts that were still remotely white were the very tops of the bands, which barely managed to keep the socks upright on Mercy's feet. Very gently, she grabbed one band and pulled down the sock.

She took in a sharp hiss of air. Fuzz from the sock had become caked in blood from wounds, and so peeled painfully away. As Mercy took off the other sock and looked at her feet, she recalled her time in the ER. It could have been worse.

With all the blood and dirt that had penetrated the socks, as well as the darkness, Mercy couldn't properly assess her injuries. Still, she carefully ran her fingers over the flesh of her feet, and determined where the truly bad spots were. There was a particularly large chunk of skin sliced open along the ball of her right foot. It seemed to be the worst of her injuries, causing the most pain.

Mercy looked around herself but didn't find anything useful. If the forest had been in full summer dress, she would have packed some green leaves around her feet. As it was, all the leaves were brown and dead. There was a bit of grass growing here and there but not much. A few ferns were budding, their ends all curled up upon themselves in hard little nubs. Giving up, Mercy put her socks back on, being extra careful with the wounded areas.

Now that she was fully aware of how badly hurt her feet were, Mercy limped as she walked. She favoured her right foot, although she wished she could just lift up both of them and float along through the woods. She tried to pick out flat rocks in her path to step on, as they didn't hurt as much. Most of the time, however, she had no choice, and found herself stepping on and over branches. The prickly bushes were the worst. Stepping over or through them always hurt the bottoms of her feet and caused a cascade of needles to drop. The needles were always trying to poke through the wooly socks, and sometimes they succeeded. Even walking around the prickly bushes was annoying, as just brushing into them caused the needles to drop. At times, Mercy walked too closely to trees with dried-out branches. They would snatch at her hair and clothes and then break off with a hollow *snap*. Every time that happened, her very first thought was that she had been shot at again. After quickly determining she hadn't been, she would pause to search the area for flashlights.

Mercy had seen the flashlights a handful of times. They were always far enough off for her not to feel like she was in imminent danger, but she always changed her direction when they appeared. She no longer knew which way she was going in relation to her parents' house. She also didn't know if she was seeing the same man who was tracking her, or if they were all out there, spread out, trying to surround her.

It wasn't too long before another rest break was in order. Not only were Mercy's feet sore, but she was just so tired. Without a watch or her cell phone, she had no idea what time it was. Since the whole ordeal had started it could've been minutes or hours; her concept of time was completely gone. Not only was she tired, but she was hungry and thirsty too. Dinner seemed like days ago, and her stomach rumbled, complaining about its lack of contents.

The cold was the worst, though. As the night wore on, it got colder and colder. Her dad's sweater wasn't warm enough, and her sister's pajama pants even less so. As Mercy took her break, she curled her legs up and tucked them in under the sweater. She wasn't shivering yet, but that probably wasn't far off. She pulled her arms in out of the sleeves and wrapped them around her knees. If she wasn't so afraid of being found, she would have pulled her head into the sweater as well, using her breath to help warm her. The wound on her cheek made it stiff, and it was colder than the rest of her face. She raised her hands up through the shirt's collar and exhaled into them, using her hot breath to warm both them and her lips. It was then that she noticed she could see her breath when breathing normally. What had the weatherman said the temperature would drop down to tonight? Mercy couldn't recall. It would be low though. This early in the spring the nights were still cold, and could even bring frost. If it had been summer, the cold wouldn't have been a problem.

"Ifs and buts," Mercy whispered to her fingers.

A light appeared in the distance. One of the men was near. Mercy stood up, keeping her arms tucked in closely to her body, and started walking again.

A song was stuck in her head. Actually, it was the song that the truck had been blasting at the house. It repeated over and over in Mercy's mind, trying to drive her insane. She didn't even know all the lyrics—that was the worst part—just a snatch of the main chorus looping forever.

Her repeating thoughts were interrupted by a sound. It wasn't a threatening sound, however. Mercy recognized the rush of running water. She must be somewhere near the river that ran through the woods. She knew the river. If she got there, she would know where she was and which way to go.

It took Mercy longer than she hoped to pin down the direction of the sound. A few times she wandered off-course, and when the sound became quieter, she would redirect herself. It would be so nice to reach the river. Not only would she finally have her bearings, but she could also wash the wounds on her feet and take a much-needed drink. The river water wasn't exactly the cleanest, but it was better than nothing.

She climbed up to the top of a hill and looked down. There, running through a deep valley in the land, was the river. Mercy began her careful descent, grabbing onto trees and branches when she didn't feel stable enough. The ground soon turned to rock and she had to scramble along using both her hands and feet. At last she was on the shore. Looking up and down the banks, she instantly knew where she was.

Just downstream from Mercy, the river was spanned by a wooden bridge. It was high, crossing from the top edge of one side of the valley to the other. It was the shore on the other side of that bridge that Mercy knew well. She, her family, and friends would ride up to the bridge, park, and take a trail down the other side. The river pooled on the downstream side of the bridge and was an excellent water hole for those hot summer days. Upstream, where Mercy was currently perched, were all large chunks of jagged rock. Even further up, the valley became a pair of cliff sides before sloping back into gentle hills.

Mercy picked her way around the rocks until she was able to reach the edge of the water. She found a stable, mostly flat rock and rested upon it. Taking the socks off again was painful. Her feet were even redder and angrier-looking than before. She rolled up her pant legs, and slowly dipped her feet into the water.

It was like ice, and Mercy quickly withdrew her feet. She had forgotten how cold the water still was at this time of year. Steeling herself against it, she dipped her feet into the river again.

Her feet were numb in moments. The numbness was actually rather nice. Mercy then dipped her hands in and began rubbing the dirt and blood off her feet. Her hands were also quickly numbed.

Clomp, clomp, clomp.

Mercy raised her head, looking toward the bridge. Her overly-alert senses had just been able to pick up the sound over that of the river. Heavy boots trod along the wood, their owner carrying a flashlight. Mercy was able to recognize him as cat mask by the pointed ears.

He went to the middle of the bridge and started searching the river.

CHAPTER NINE

Mercy's teeth started to chatter as the water reached up to her rib cage. When cat mask had started to search the river, she hadn't had enough time to scramble back to a place where the rocks or trees would hide her. The only option she saw was the one that lay directly in front of her. She slid into the cold depths.

The river wasn't deep where she was. Mercy's feet touched the slimy bottom, and she was able to walk the few steps to a large, triangular boulder that jutted out above the surface. With her socks on her hands, she pressed herself against the back of the rock, which was just tall enough to hide her from view.

Mercy shivered against her shield, hoping the natural flow of the water hid the ripples her trembling caused. Her heart was hammering again, like a caged beast trying to escape. It gave her something to focus on, something other than the cold. She saw the water around her hiding place get brighter as the edges of the flashlight beam swept over it. Instinctively she pressed herself tighter to the rock.

The light drifted away from her, toward the far shore. She watched as the circle of light scanned up the steep hillside, lingering on certain rocks and trees more than others. It then came back toward her, and Mercy squeezed her eyes shut as it passed by. She turned her head and watched as the light scanned her side of the river. It paused for a moment where she had sat. Mercy thought that maybe she had left behind some indication that she had been there. She couldn't see anything from her present angle, however, and the light didn't linger long.

She sighed with relief and accidentally slid a little bit more into the water because of it. Beneath her feet, the bottom was slippery with algae. They weren't as slippery as her usual swimming spot, because the water here was faster, but it was still hard to get a perfect grip. If the water had been higher, she would have just let the current push her into the boulder she hid behind, but it was too shallow, so she had to stand. Mercy found slightly better footing, the wounds on her feet reminding her of their presence as they got pushed against the rocks.

The light moved off to somewhere Mercy couldn't see. Taking a risk, she shifted to one side and peered around her hiding spot. Cat mask was checking out the other side of the river now.

Mercy debated with herself about whether she should try to get out of the river right now, or if swimming down it would be a better idea. Out of the river she had more mobility options, but if she swam downstream, she could hide under the bridge, where the men might not think to check. As Mercy seriously considered getting out of the water while cat mask wasn't looking, even going so far as to scope out a good outcrop of rocks across the way, another man showed up.

His flashlight was off, and Mercy wasn't aware of his presence until he stepped onto the bridge. She quickly ducked back behind the rock, but it was only a second later that she peered out again. Judging by the size of the man, she guessed it was rat mask.

The cat and rat appeared to be conversing about something. The distance, their low voices, and the burbling of the river all attributed to Mercy being unable to hear exactly what they were saying. She silently wished that she could read lips, although it wasn't like she could make out their lips in the dark.

After a minute, the third man, the rabbit, showed up. He joined the other two on the bridge, flicking off his flashlight so that only the cat's was on. The rabbit appeared cold, rubbing his arms and shifting from foot to foot.

Mercy seethed at him. He didn't know cold. Sitting in this river, now that was cold. Although it warmed for a moment when Mercy's bladder relieved itself. She hadn't realized just how full it had been until the problem took care of itself on its own.

The rat man cuffed the rabbit's head for some reason, and then pushed on the cat's shoulder. They weren't perfectly harmonious but they were still working together well enough to keep Mercy very afraid.

After several more excruciating minutes of conversation, the group of men finished talking. They crossed the bridge and split up. The cat went up river, the rabbit went down, and the rat must have continued following the path, although Mercy couldn't see him anymore.

She focused on the cat. He was walking along the ridgeline, slowly, toward Mercy. His flashlight scanned from the trees to the river and back again. As he got closer and closer, Mercy slowly shifted along the rock. She kept the big boulder between them at all times. It made Mercy think of playing tag with her siblings. The one who wasn't 'it' would run around the dining room table and then keep it between him or her and 'it'. As long as the table was kept between the two, it was impossible for 'it' to tag the other. In the end, 'it' would usually crawl under the table, which gave the other time to get away, or 'it' would just leave to chase the remaining sibling.

This time it wasn't a game. And 'it' wanted to kill her, not tag her. She had to make sure he couldn't see her, especially with that shotgun of his. If he found out where she was, it would be like shooting fish in a barrel. Hell, he might even take out a few fish with Mercy in the process; she had felt maybe one or two brush against her ankles while she had been standing there. At least she thought she did, it was impossible to tell what with the numbness of her feet.

Mercy completely hid beside the rock as the cat got nearer. She squeezed her eyes shut again when she thought the light might be passing over where she was. She stood there, eyes closed, body pressed to the rock. She waited until she was certain that cat mask must be near the cliffs before opening her eyes again. He was heading up toward the top of them, being leery of the edge in case it wasn't stable. As he got up higher, he started to check the river and the banks less frequently.

In that area, there was nowhere for Mercy to hide and nothing for her to hold onto.

She finally moved away from the boulder and went to shore. She climbed out the same place she had slid in. Her legs were numb and weak with cold, her knees knocking together. When she finally got her feet up on the rock with her, they were as pale as snow where the wounds weren't making them a standout pink and red. Even some of the scratches had lost their colour due to the cold. Her skin was jumping, twitching, and shuddering, while goose bumps carpeted it.

Although still thirsty, Mercy realized it would be a bad idea to drink too much of the cold water. She leaned over and took a single swallow, soothing her sore throat. She then took another gulp and held that one in her mouth for as long as possible; trying to trick her mind into thinking it got more water than it did.

By rubbing her feet, Mercy hoped to get feeling back into them. She would have liked to leave the riverside right away, but in her current condition, she would have just fallen over. Eventually she was able to scramble up a few rocks to a slightly more sheltered position. There, she rubbed her feet again. With her pajama pants soaked, there was no way to get her feet completely dry, so she got them as dry as she could and put the socks back on. She shivered and shook the whole way up the steep hill.

When she reached the top, Mercy made her way to the dirt road that led to the bridge. She approached it slowly. Although she would have heard if one of the men crossed the bridge again in their big boots, she couldn't be sure that they hadn't taken off their boots and doubled back. Or maybe the rat was just standing on the other side of the bridge, watching.

At the edge of the road, Mercy slowly stuck her head out from around a tree. She looked to the bridge first and saw no one there. Under the skeletal trees across the span it was very dark and hard to see, but if there was anyone there, it was unlikely they'd be able to see Mercy under her own bone-like branches. Along the road in the other direction, she didn't see anyone either. Mercy stepped out onto the path. She paused there a moment, expecting to get shot for being out in the open. When she wasn't, she started down the road.

At first Mercy walked, her shoulders hunched, her arms wrapped around her chest, trying to regain some warmth. Her knees were practically knocking together with every step, her drenched clothing leaving a trail of drips behind her. She worried about the dripping at first, but then she realized that the earth was absorbing the droplets rather quickly. She had probably left a more obvious trail on the rocks where she had climbed out. The dirt road was soft, with patches of grass sprouting up here and there. It hadn't been used in a while; at least not since the winter snow had melted away.

After a short time, Mercy began to jog. It hurt her feet, but not nearly as badly as running through the forest had. She didn't have to watch her step so much, or worry about branches grasping at her. The jogging helped stimulate her blood flow, which warmed her up a bit. She wished she had a hat. The breeze her jogging created made her ears cold, and she knew that would eventually lead to a headache.

Screw the headache, Mercy just needed to get the hell out of there. She wanted to get back to civilization, back to where she could use a telephone and call for help. Somewhere where these men in masks couldn't find her.

To keep her earlier earworm at bay, Mercy kept her mind occupied by planning out exactly what she would do once she had a phone. The first thing would be to call the police; that part was obvious. After that, she would call Kenny. She would give anything to hear his voice right now, reassuring her, telling her that everything would be okay. After that, a long, steamy, hot shower sounded great. It would wash the night off her and warm her bones. Then she would crawl into her bed, back home at her apartment. On second thought, maybe getting new locks put in before that would be a better idea: ones that weren't easy to pick. Then, sometime after that, she'd call her parents and tell them what had happened. It wasn't a call that Mercy particularly looked forward to making. It would be high-strung and full of emotion, but she didn't want them just going home, seeing the mess, and wondering.

When she came to a fork in the road, Mercy had to stop jogging and take a moment to remember which way led where. While she stopped, she decided to look around her, to see if any flashlight beams were in sight. None were; the woods were dark. Her feet were throbbing. Deciding to take it easy on them, Mercy started walking again. She was slightly warmer now, although her skin kept up a steady covering of goose flesh.

The closer she got to the edge of the woods, the more nervous Mercy became. A part of her was elated that this night would finally end, but a seed of doubt nagged at her. She felt she was missing something.

When she knew the house was near, she stepped off the path. Mercy picked her way through the trees, stepping carefully. She kept expecting to see a flashlight beam appear at any moment. She didn't.

Mercy popped out of the trees into the field across the street from the house. She got down and crawled the rest of the way out of the woods, and then lay on her stomach in the wild grass. She watched the house from across the road. It was dark and empty. Nothing moved inside. The truck still sat in front, parked on the lawn, the high beams finally turned off. Her own car sat in the driveway.

She debated whether going to the house was worth it. There was no way to contact the police from inside, but there were clean, dry, and warm clothes she could change into. In the end, the prospect of driving to the Abrams' seemed like a much more appealing alternative to walking.

After waiting another minute without seeing movement, Mercy got up to her feet. She walked through the ankle-high grass, staying close to the trees in case she needed to make a quick escape. The only sounds were her legs brushing through the grass, and cricket song. She paused where the road ended and the dirt paths through the forest began. Checking once more for flashlights and seeing none, she scurried across.

She approached the truck first. There were no markings on it to distinguish a brand, and Mercy didn't know enough about pickup trucks to tell very much from the size and shape. It was black, maybe even a dark blue or dark green, the low lighting making it difficult to be certain. There were no license plates. Like the hood-ornament they had been removed, leaving only holes where things were supposed to be bolted on. Mercy approached the bed of the truck. The pickup had large, off-road tires, which she used to step up. The pickup's bed was empty, just a few pebbles and flakes of dirt sat along the bottom. Stepping off the tire and peeking in through the driver's window, Mercy saw a simple interior. A part of her had been expecting a pigsty, with beer bottles and take-out containers littered about the place. It surprised her that there wasn't even a cigarette butt lying somewhere. The only thing that didn't look standard was the police scanner. At least that explained how they knew she hadn't called the cops. Mercy looked in at the rear seats through the other windows and found the same, plain interior. Trying the handles, she found all the doors to be locked. Cat mask or someone else had probably taken the keys with him. Either way, there was nothing Mercy could learn about her attackers from the truck.

The door to the house stood open. Mercy walked inside, hesitant, like it was she who was the intruder. Her coat still hung on the rack near the door, the keys within a pocket. She grabbed the coat, pulling it on over her chilly shoulders, and quickly backed out through the door again. The house wasn't as inviting as it had been upon arrival.

Mercy just wanted to get to the Abram place; she didn't care about her wet pajama pants anymore. She could warm up over there while calling the police.

Unlocking her car door, she slid behind the wheel and jammed the key into the ignition. She turned the key. Nothing happened.

"Oh, come on, don't do this," Mercy whispered and pleaded with her car. She turned the key again and still nothing. It didn't even try to turn over. Tears sprouted out of the corners of her eyes.

Suddenly getting an idea as to what might be wrong, Mercy pulled on the hood release. She got out and went around to the front of her car. There, she lifted up the hood and looked inside. Without a light source better than the stars, it was nearly impossible to make out any details about the engine, but there was an obvious black hole in one section. Mercy reached her hand forward and waved it around in the hole, confirming there was nothing there. Her battery was gone.

Angry, Mercy slammed down the hood. She immediately regretted her action as the sound carried out across the fields and into the woods. Her own strung-out nerves caused her to crouch and cower against the front bumper of her car as if shot at. The crickets had fallen silent for a moment due to the sudden noise, but they began their chirping again soon enough.

Realizing she would have to walk, Mercy got up and scurried back toward the house. Just inside the door sat her sneakers. She picked them up, grateful for the fact that she had worn them instead of her sandals. If she had been going anywhere other than her parents' house, she wouldn't have been caught dead wearing her sneakers with her sundress. Her parents and siblings didn't care about fashion, however, and so she had opted for the sneakers that were more comfortable for driving.

Carrying her shoes by their laces in one hand and her keys in the other, Mercy hurried into the TV room. She was going to quickly change out of her wet clothes, maybe bandage her feet, and then get to the Abrams'. As she passed through the room, she began to feel ill at ease. Something seemed off, but she couldn't tell what it was. Maybe it was just the lack of life in the house what with the power out and nobody home. Or maybe it was that the door to the office was open with nothing but a black void beyond it.

When she entered the reading room, Mercy figured it out. The flashlight that should have been on and plugged into the wall, was not. The reading room was much darker than it should have been. As Mercy thought about it, she couldn't recall seeing the one in the living room turned on either. She remembered thinking about how dark the house was. Why were the flashlights gone? There was no way her pursuers in the woods would've unplugged them before giving chase. Maybe they took them while she had been running around upstairs. But why? That made no sense to Mercy.

A floorboard behind her creaked.

CHAPTER TEN

MERCY REACTED IN A way she hadn't expected. A part of her brain thought it was strange that she threw herself forward, instead of turning around. It thought this while she was doing it, like a passenger in her own body who was observing things at a slower rate. She didn't turn until her arms reached the bookshelves.

Behind her, a man was grunting, having just missed grabbing her and throwing himself off-balance in the process. He quickly became upright again and lunged for Mercy.

She swung her shoes like a club, connecting with the side of the man's head. He grunted in surprise, but didn't stop. Mercy was slammed into the bookcase, one of the wooden shelves digging painfully into the small of her back. The slap with the shoes had knocked the man's mask askew, and he couldn't see what part of Mercy he was trying to grab. Mercy swung her other arm around and brought down her keys. That passenger part of her brain wondered why she had still been holding onto them. Her car key dug into the meaty flesh of the attacker's arm.

The man cried out in pain and backed away. He ripped the key out, tossed it away, and fixed his mask. He wore the mask of a wolf.

Mercy made for the kitchen, but the man grabbed her coat sleeve. In one fluid motion, she slipped out of the jacket and whacked the man with her shoes again. Once free of the fabric that the man had grabbed, Mercy found herself next to another bookcase. Frantically, she grabbed book after book, and threw them at the wolf.

He raised his arms to defend his head, as one of the books met its target. He bellowed out in anger and tried to get to Mercy again. His foot landed on one of the fallen books, however, and he slipped. The wolf almost managed to stay upright, but he hadn't noticed the footrest where he wanted to put his other leg, and ended up tumbling over. He hit the floor with a hard smack.

Mercy dashed out of the room, able to hear the wolf scrambling to his feet behind her. As she reached the kitchen through the swinging door, the passenger section of her brain knew that she would never reach the back door in time. Even if she reached the door, the man behind her would just pounce upon her outside. She turned instead.

The door to the dumbwaiter into the basement was open and Mercy threw herself inside. The compartment was tiny, and as the man came through the swinging door, he easily spotted her legs being pulled in.

Mercy started screaming and kicking as the wolf reached for her feet. The fabric of her silky pajama pants was too slick with damp for the wolf to get a good grip as her legs thrashed about. They fought for only seconds before all of Mercy's movements and weight were too much for the dumbwaiter. Both of them heard the rope snap.

Sucking her feet in just in time, Mercy watched her view of the man quickly shrink. His arms had followed after her though, and the dumbwaiter was slammed to a stop. The wolf roared out in pain as his forearms were trapped between the top of the dumbwaiter and lower edge of the wall opening.

His fingers and wrists thrashed, still trying to grab Mercy. She cried out as he managed to rip out a chuck of her hair. Mercy began to fight back in the tiny space, clawing at the groping hands with her own. The wolf stopped trying to grab her. Instead, he placed the palms of his hands against the top of the dumbwaiter and started lifting it back up with considerable strength.

Mercy shook and battered at the sides of the small box, trying to make it harder for him. As more of the kitchen came into view, she panicked. Craning her neck up, Mercy was able to bite one of the wolf's fingers. He screamed and quickly yanked his hands out of the dumbwaiter. Mercy plummeted, no longer supported by anything.

She hit the bottom of the shaft, her body bouncing around in the tiny compartment. By tomorrow she would feel like one large bruise. Mercy launched herself out of the little box, falling to the floor and scraping her palms. Her mouth tasted of blood but she couldn't be sure if it was the wolf's or her own. She quickly sprang back up to her feet, her shoes still dangling from one hand. It was nearly pitch black. Mercy was in the wine cellar section of the basement where there were no windows.

A thunder rolled down the stairs as the wolf came after her. A flashlight blazed to life, piercing through the darkness and illuminating where Mercy stood. The wolf left the light on a table so that it pointed at her, and then started running straight at her.

Mercy grabbed the nearest bottle of wine and threw it. It missed, shattering on the cement floor and releasing a powerful aroma. The second one struck his arm. It didn't break, but it slowed him down. The third one wasn't even thrown. Mercy brought the bottle down on his shoulder as he slammed her against the wall. Both of them collapsed to the floor.

As the two of them tried to get up, Mercy began flailing with her shoes again. She struck the wolf a few times, just enough to get him to raise his arms to protect his head. It gave Mercy the opportunity to get to her feet before he could. She started to cross the basement, but the wolf lunged at her from the ground, grabbing her ankles. Mercy fell, striking her chin on the cement and seeing stars explode before her eyes. During her brief moment of being stunned, the wolf got to his feet.

As Mercy tried to get up and get away, he grabbed her around the waist, pressing her back against his stomach. Screaming so loudly it hurt her throat, she starting swinging her elbows and kicking her feet. She was wriggling and wrenching her body like a hellcat, the man barely able to hold on amidst the blows that landed. One elbow managed to find its way into his ribs, his lungs exhaling with a whoosh.

Mercy then clawed at the arms encircling her, while her heels struck him in the shins. She managed to get one of her legs high enough to throw it into his crotch.

They both went down again, and they both cried out in pain. They had landed on the broken wine bottle.

Mercy pushed herself over onto her side, no longer held down. A shard of glass protruded from her left knee. The wolf rolled onto his back and yanked a considerably larger chunk of glass out of his side, tossing it at the washing machine. The piece of glass consisted of most of the wine bottle's base and bounced off the machine with a hollow *bong*. Unable to bend her leg, Mercy used her other three limbs to start dragging herself toward the nearby worktable. The wolf lunged after her again, again grabbing hold of her ankles.

He planted his knees on the cement, a piece of glass breaking with a pop beneath one, and dragged Mercy to him. What he hadn't noticed was that Mercy had been able to reach the worktable. She quickly rolled onto her back, a handsaw gripped tightly. She swung the saw at his face, but was unable to turn the sharp side toward him in time. Still, the large, flat side hit him with a *whap*. The wolf's head rocked to one side, his mask, made crooked again, barely managed to stay on his face. He held onto Mercy though, and tried to yank her upright.

Mercy followed through with his pull. With her free hand, she grabbed at the wolf's face, using his mask to pull herself even further forward. She got right up on her knees, howling with pain from the glass in one, and threw herself past the wolf's side.

The saw came down right into the back of his knee.

There was a moment, a split second, when Mercy was looking at the unmasked wolf. They were looking each other right in the eye. She, lying partly on her side behind him, and he, kneeling, his body twisting to face her. His eyes held fear and pain. Then she pulled hard on the saw, the blade slicing through his jeans, through his skin, through his tendons, and grating along the bones.

Never, not even during her stint in the ER, had Mercy heard such a feral and agonizing scream.

The wolf dropped to his side instantly, reaching for his wounded leg. Mercy scrambled to her feet, almost falling back over when she put weight on her own injured knee. Picking up her fallen shoes, and with the saw blade still in hand, she hobbled toward the steps. Upon reaching the stairs, she half-sat, half-collapsed on them, looking back at the wolf. He no longer screamed, but whimpered, tears running from his eyes. Mercy felt no remorse. He had grabbed a few articles of clothing from the pile that Mercy had dropped down earlier, and was gingerly holding them to the back of his leg, trying to staunch the blood flow. He even found a belt to use as a tourniquet.

With her long sleeve wrapped around her fingers to protect them, Mercy yanked the piece of glass out of her own knee, whimpering herself. It started bleeding, but it didn't look too bad. She didn't think any major arteries were hit.

The wolf started moving again. Mercy snapped up to her feet, holding the saw out threateningly. Looking into her eyes, the wolf reached into one of his pockets. He pulled out a small walkie-talkie and pressed a button on the side.

"She's in the house," he spoke harshly into the device. He then grinned at Mercy, his teeth shining eerily white in the flashlight beam.

Mercy quickly turned away from him. She hobbled her way up the steps, using the railing for support. At the top, she risked putting even more weight on her knee to get out through the back door. The saw was still clutched in her hand.

Outside once more, Mercy made her way to the sheep fence. She hauled herself up and over it, grateful that Mr. Abram hadn't used any barbed wire.

CHAPTER ELEVEN

SLIDING HER FEET INTO her shoes was an awful experience. Not only was the initial pressure on the wounds terrible, but her gashed-open knee was still a throbbing ball of pain and was already stiffening on her.

Mercy was sitting on the side of a hill in the sheep meadow, the house out of sight behind her. She figured it was safe to stop there and put on her shoes because it would take awhile for the other men to reach the house, especially if they were still beyond the river when the wolf had radioed them.

As she tied up the laces, Mercy kept picturing the face of the wolf beneath the mask. She wanted to remember every detail, so that if they got away before the police arrived, she'd be able to give a perfect description. She remembered the way the beam of the flashlight reflected off his bright brown eyes right before she pulled on the saw blade. They were almost honey-coloured. He also had shaggy auburn hair that covered the tops of his ears, and a mole on his neck, just below the jaw on the right side. He didn't have a soft jawline, but Mercy wouldn't have called it square either. His face was surprisingly open for a man trying to kill her, with large, wide-set eyes, and thin lips. If she had walked past him on the street, she probably wouldn't have given him a second glance. Thinking about the phone calls, she realized she might have actually passed him on the street at some point. It was impossible to know for sure just how long they had been watching her.

With her shoes tied up, Mercy took a look at her knee through the hole in her pants. It had mostly stopped bleeding, but was still oozing in some spots. Regretting the fact that she had left her jacket behind, Mercy pulled off her sweater. She tied it tightly around her knee and got to her feet.

It was still cold. Mercy's breaths came out of her in puffs. She pulled one of her arms into her T-shirt. The other, she pulled in most of the way, but left her hand poking out like a weird T-rex arm to hold onto the saw. Constantly rubbing her forearms together like the crickets rubbing their legs, she continued her journey across the fields.

Travelling uphill was the worst. Her bad knee could only hold her weight for a second on level ground, so when going up, she was basically hopping. And although the shoes helped a lot, her feet were still fairly tender. Downhill was better, but not by much; Mercy greatly preferred the even stretches.

Shivering, shaking, and limping, Mercy made her slow way toward the Abram home. She often checked behind her, or looked toward where the road lay, her eyes seeking out some form of light. She never saw anything other than what the far away starlight revealed. Of all nights for the moon to be gone.

The few times she had spotted movement on the hills and in the valleys, she would stop. So far, it had just been sheep. Most of the sheep would trot off when they spotted her, heading back to where the rest of flock was huddling for the night. The weak part of Mercy wanted to go find the flock. Again she just wanted to lie down and sleep, this time among the sheep. She imagined the heat their bodies gave off would be pleasant.

A steep hill rose in front of her. Mercy began to climb it, but her limbs weakened and her knee cried out just after she had begun. She laid the saw down in the grass and then laid herself down next to it. She breathed in the cold scent of the greenery beside her face, feeling the beginnings of frost on the blades beneath her cheek.

"Ifs and buts," Mercy muttered. Her lips were cold and chapped. "If only you had gone fishing with Kenny."

She imagined what Kenny would be doing right now. He was probably sleeping in the cabin, Roofus lying on the floor next to him, snoring. Roofus had a tendency to snore whenever he got a lot of exercise. After being out in the woods, he would be sawing wood tonight. There was a chance that Kenny was snoring too. Although it didn't happen often, drink usually brought it on. Without any women around, the boys had probably gotten recklessly drunk off their asses.

Mercy figured they had probably caught some fish that day and had them for dinner. The cabin would smell strongly of both fish and alcohol. A fire would have been burning in the fireplace, a much more pleasant aroma. It would likely be ash by this time, but the warmth of it would linger awhile longer.

In the morning, the boys would wake up, hungover. They would cook a breakfast consisting of eggs, bacon, and sausages. Maybe even fish, if there was any left over. Roofus would get the scraps of their meal, even though Mercy had told Kenny not to give him any people food. Kenny would do that sometimes. He would deliberately disobey Mercy if he thought the happiness of another would balance out her annoyance.

She would get silent payback though. Roofus would pay them back for her. Human food always gave Roofus gas, and they would be trapped in the car with him on the long ride home.

"Baaaaah!"

Mercy's eyes flew open. She was still lying on the hillside, unsure if she had fallen asleep or not. There was no way to determine the passage of time.

A sheep walked past her, within touching distance, climbing up the hill. She watched its upward journey, jealous of the ease with which it walked. Pushing with her arms, Mercy got up on her one good knee. Looking up at the hill before her, she decided that it would be far easier to crawl up the thing than to try walking.

Inch by inch, Mercy wormed her way up the hill, dragging her saw behind her. She was still shivering, which Mercy took to be a good sign. If she stopped, then she knew death wouldn't be too far off. Her eyes burned with exhaustion. They were constantly pried wide with pain. Sleep was the only thing that would make the pain in her eyes go away, but for now, it helped her keep them open.

The sheep was gone, but Mercy pressed on. She wasn't going to let some damn sheep show her up, no siree bob.

As she finally clawed her way over the upper edge of the hill, she once more collapsed into the grass. Her skin was pale, and covered in a fine sheen of sweat. It made the cold worse. With her skin shuddering and jiving all over the place, she managed to drag herself up into a sitting position. The other side of the hill sloped away about three feet in front of her, and there, across some blessedly flat land, she could see the Abrams' house.

It was a smaller home than her parents' place up the road. It was a one-storey cottage, which Mercy remembered as being quite spacious inside. Each child in the family had their own small bedroom that opened onto the central space, which was both a living room and a kitchen mashed together. Along the front of the house was a large screened-in porch, the sides of which connected to the sheep fence, making the home part of the barricade. Mercy remembered many nights when her family had walked or ridden bicycles down the road to play cards with the Abrams in that porch, safe from the bugs outside. The kids would have moved out by now, or at least most of them would have. Mercy was fairly certain there was at least one boy left helping out his dad with the farm.

The sheep were currently milling about behind the house, between it and the barn. The barn was old and rickety, serving only as a storage facility for the shearing tools and the bundles of wool. Mercy wasn't surprised that the sheep would gather here. Mr. Abram was a man of routine; he fed the sheep from the same troughs every day, always at sunrise. The sheep were probably waiting for the sun and their morning meal. Mercy wondered how long they would have to wait.

A single light burned in the Abram home. An electric lamp shone brightly next to the front door. They had electricity.

Mercy crawled to the edge of the hill, saw in hand once more. The far side down was just as steep as the side she had climbed. With her teeth chattering, she lay on her side and slowly slid down. A few times her bad leg would hit the ground and send a jarring bolt of pain up from her knee. Mercy just gritted her teeth as much as the shivering let her and carried on.

The farther down the hill she got, the more everything smelled like sheep. Out in the fields, the scent was better dispersed, but down here, where they congregated the most, it became heavy and cloying. The Abram kids always had the faint smell of sheep on them. Mercy remembered her grandfather had always smelled like that too, and so associated it with pleasant things.

Finally reaching the bottom of the hill, she struggled to get up onto her feet. Her body was having a hell of a time listening to her brain. Cold, exhausted, and injured, it seemed like everything was working against her. Still, her goal was in sight.

Mercy hobbled toward the back door of the house, which was closer to her than the front. She had to pass through the flock of sheep in the process. Most of the sheep were silent and still, trying to get some shut-eye. Mercy bumped into them, swatting at them with the flat side of the saw from time to time to get them moving. They *baa'd* at her with indignation. A few of the sheep moved away by themselves. The way their flanks jittered nervously, Mercy suspected it was the smell of blood on her that caused them to move.

Finally through, Mercy reached the back door. It was a simple screen door with a heavier wooden one beyond it. She pulled open the screen door, the hinges creaking loudly, to knock on the wooden one.

"Hello." She'd tried to cry out but instead produced a horse rasp. "Mr. and Mrs. Abram?"

There was no answer. Mercy knocked louder, putting all the effort she had left into it.

"Hello," she managed to call louder this time. "It's Mercy Chalmers. Please, I know it's late, but I need help."

She rested her forehead against the wood, an energy-sapping wave passing over her. She had a thought then: what if they weren't home? Mercy suddenly pictured Mrs. Abram trying to call her, wanting an update on little Robin. She could imagine the old woman demanding that her husband—or son if one of them was indeed still there—drive her all the way into the city to check on the boy. Mrs. Abram could be unpredictable like that sometimes. Maybe Mercy's mom had even called them, and invited them to stay in the hotel with them for support.

Mercy raised her hand and wrapped it around the doorknob. She turned it and found that the door was unlocked. People out here didn't see a need to lock their doors very often. She pushed the door in, its own hinges squeaking half as loudly as the screen door's.

"Mr. and Mrs. Abram?" Mercy called out again. There was no answer. They must have gone out.

Mercy found the light switch next to the door and flipped it up. The kitchen and living room area looked as tidy as she remembered. She very quickly spotted the telephone attached to the wall near the fridge and headed for it. As she did, she glanced sideways, and saw through an open doorway.

She stopped dead in her tracks when she spotted a ghastly woman looking back at her.

CHAPTER TWELVE

MERCY HAD STARTLED HERSELF. What she thought was a frightful woman, was in fact, her own reflection in the bathroom mirror. Stunned by her appearance, Mercy walked toward it. Her eyes were wide, hollow, red-rimmed, and had dark smudges beneath them. She was covered in dirt; the only clean spots were the tracks her tears had made down her cheeks. What skin she could see on her arms and face was either as pale as the missing moon, or an angry red from injury. Her hair was a tangled snarl and she could see where the wolf had ripped out a chunk. Her lips were drained of colour, turning blue.

As she neared the bathroom, a terrible smell assaulted Mercy's nose. She scrunched it up and took a step back, raising the back of her hand to her face. There was something familiar about the smell. It wasn't coming from the bathroom, but from the room next door: Mr. and Mrs. Abram's bedroom.

Mercy walked up to the door and pushed on it. It wasn't latched and swung easily inward. The smell got ten times worse. Mercy gasped as the light from the main room flooded in through the open door and revealed its grisly occupants.

The Abrams were dead. Butchered. The old couple lay on the bed together, blood soaking into everything. There were cuts in the bodies so deep that white bone was showing. Absurdly, Mercy's eyes focused on the surgical screws that had been placed in Mrs. Abram's tibia bone. She had badly broken the leg when a sheep knocked her off balance, and she had fallen down one of the hills outside.

Mercy tore her eyes away, forcing them downward. On the floor was another man, probably one of the Abram's sons. He had been gutted. His entrails lay spread across the rug as if someone had been trying to untangle a ball of Christmas lights. It was likely that the son had heard something going on in his parents' room, and had gone to check it out. He had been met by the same fate.

She took a step into the room. As a nurse, her mind wanted to check on them, make sure that they were, in fact, dead. She wanted to help the Abrams. It was clearly too late for that though. Sshe knew why she recognized the smell. Blood, feces, and the beginnings of decay: all things she had dealt with in the work place.

Fresh tears sprung to her eyes, but these were the red-hot tears of anger. The Abrams hadn't deserved this. No one deserved this save the men who would do such a thing. She gripped her saw tightly and turned away from the slaughter.

A man was in the living room section of the space. He was tall, and wearing the upper half of a rubber bird mask. An eagle or hawk of some sort. Unlike his compatriots wearing hoodies, this man wore a black T-shirt. His arms were thin, but well-muscled. His jeans were covered in dark stains. His hands had dried blood on them, and in one of them he held a large combat knife.

Mercy stood her ground, staring down the man across the space. Through the holes in his mask, his eyes were dark, flat, and uncaring.

"You must be Mercy Chalmers." His voice was unexpectedly high-pitched for one so tall. It was a bit feminine, not gruff or grating like Mercy had expected. There was an airy quality to it, and his tone made him sound as if he were speaking from a far-off place inside his own mind.

Mercy didn't answer. She clenched the saw tighter, her fingers hurting from their severe contraction around the grip.

"I wasn't supposed to see you tonight," the bird continued speaking. "The others were supposed to deal with you. Tell me, why did they fail?"

This man was clearly a little bit nuts. Mercy feared that that meant she was in more danger than she at first thought. A rational killer seemed like an easier one to deal with than an irrational one.

The man's eyes drifted down and then back up, taking in Mercy's entire appearance. They lingered briefly on the bloodied saw before returning to look her directly in the eyes again.

"Ah, you cut one of them did you? Which one?" He didn't sound upset, merely curious. Intrigued even.

"The wolf," Mercy told him, her voice sounding a lot harsher than his.

"I never did like him." What might pass for a smile briefly alighted on the bird's lips, before disappearing again. "He bites." The bird snapped his teeth. "Tell me, did he bite you?"

Mercy shifted her feet slightly, her knee getting tired. She looked from the bird to the rear door and then back again. "No. He didn't bite me. He didn't even try." She didn't mention that she had bitten him.

"Good. I hate the idea of his teeth touching your lovely flesh."

The comment threw Mercy mentally off-balance. She hadn't expected a compliment, especially the way she currently looked. Although a compliment from this man seemed like a bad thing.

"I commend you for getting away," the bird continued. "Especially for managing to injure one of them in the process. Who went into the house after you? The snake?"

The snake? Mercy hadn't seen anyone wearing a snake mask. There were a lot more of these bastards than she had realized. Were there any others she was missing?

"No, the rat."

"Oh, of course. He was the one who spoke to you over the phone, yes?"

"I think so."

"Although I, myself, called you once."

Mercy's back stiffened. She would have recognized this man's voice had he called her. If he thought that he had called, then he was even crazier than Mercy was pegging him for.

"Oh don't get me wrong." The bird seemed to notice her change in posture. "I didn't speak to you."

"Were you the breather?" She couldn't hear him breathing from where she stood, but Mercy found it hard to believe that this man would be able to make that kind of sound.

"In a sense. I killed a man over the phone for you."

Mercy's mind froze, utterly confused. "What?"

"I was the third message on the machine. The rat called you first, and then the rabbit, although he hung up right away. I left you a message. I'm not sure you could hear much as the man's mouth was taped over, but I slit his throat for you."

She tried to think back to the messages she had received that first night. She remembered the rat, the first breather. With that, she remembered the one she thought was a mouth breather. She remembered thinking it had a panicked quality, but had just brushed it off as Kenny being a dick.

"Who? Who did you kill?" her voice broke.

"I believe he was best known as Dr. Lynch."

Mercy knew Dr. Lynch. He was one of the doctors who worked in conjunction with the coma ward. Specifically, he oversaw the coma cases where surgery was needed. He was a good man who was good at his job. Mercy had worked with him on several cases, even scrubbing in on a procedure or two when an extra nurse was needed to run some simple background tasks. She liked Dr. Lynch.

"I believe I've upset you," the bird commented on Mercy's change of facial expression.

Mercy wanted to snap at him. Of course he had upset her! His calm, detached way of speaking only infuriated her further.

The bird suddenly looked away from Mercy, toward the front door. He didn't say anything; he just stood there, looking out through the windows and screens and into the night.

Mercy didn't know what to make of this sudden change of focus. She glanced in the direction that he gazed, but couldn't see anything out there. The light next to the front door revealed nothing unusual. Mercy looked toward the back door. Very slowly, she took a step in its direction. The bird didn't react. Whatever he was looking at or listening to, he was completely focused on it, paying no attention to Mercy whatsoever.

She took another step toward the door, and then another. As she moved, Mercy kept her eyes on the bird, her saw held up between the two of them. If he was going to suddenly lunge at her, she would be prepared. It was tempting to go for the phone, but that was farther away, more in line with the bird's sight. It seemed unlikely that he would let her call the police while he stood right there.

Mercy reached the back door, while the bird continued to stare in the totally opposite direction. She glanced behind her, checking out through the screen door, the wooden one having been left open. She saw nothing but sheep outside. Looking back toward the bird, he continued to stand as still as a statue. Backing up, Mercy pushed the door open behind her. Even the loud squall from the hinges didn't disturb the bird. Mercy stepped backward through the door.

"Got'cha."

A black bag whisked over Mercy's head before she had time to react, a drawstring tightening around her neck. She swung wildly around with the saw, feeling it hit nothing but air.

"Whoa, Nelly!" a man's voice laughed.

She swung toward the voice but again felt nothing. Several voices were laughing now, all around her. With one hand she swung the saw wildly in all directions, trying to protect herself, while with the other, she fought to remove the black bag. The drawstring was tight around her throat, and she couldn't find a good grip to loosen it, not while swinging the saw.

The saw connected with something. A startled and pained *bah* told Mercy that it was only a sheep and not one of the men. She felt badly for the sheep, but was going to keep swinging anyway. Before she could bring the saw back around, however, something struck her in her wounded knee. The sharp explosion of pain caused her legs to give out, and she went down. Before she could react, the saw was wrenched out of her grasp, her fingers bending painfully backward.

Hands grabbed at her from everywhere. She flailed and fought but they were stronger than she was. Her wrists were brought together and she felt a coarse rope being wrapped around them. It was only a moment later that the same happened to her ankles. Still, she kicked and bucked. She clawed at her attackers, and thrashed at them, doing everything she could to inflict some sort of injury. Her own injuries were forgotten in a rush of panic-induced adrenaline.

One of the men grabbed her hooded head and clamped his hand over her mouth and nose. It was hard to breathe. Mercy screamed into the hand, fighting more than ever. There was a strange smell. Darkness, even blacker than that of the hood's interior, crept into Mercy's mind.

She began to think that this was it. This was where she was going to finally die. The sheep around her would be the only witnesses, but they wouldn't have the sense or even the means to inform anyone about what happened. They wouldn't be able to tell anyone about how she fought to the last, even when her limbs felt like immobile wooden stumps attached to her body.

Mercy knew no more.

CHAPTER THIRTEEN

Mercy was moving.

It was the first thing she realized as her consciousness swam up from the depths of her mind. Every part of her hurt, but that came secondary to the movement. She was lying on something, face up. It was hard and not flat, like some sort of corrugated metal. Whatever it was, it shuddered and shook, and occasionally even bounced. Mercy suspected she was in a vehicle of some sort. Something like the back of a pickup truck.

That's when her memories came flooding back to her. She was probably lying on the floor of the truck bed. The men in masks were driving her somewhere. She told herself to remain calm, to pretend she was still asleep. She might be able to learn some things that could help her if they thought she was still out.

Very slowly, Mercy tried to open her eyes. It wasn't until they were wide open that she realized the black bag must still be over her head. She couldn't see anything. Her wrists were still bound, resting on her chest as if in prayer. During the occasional bump, she was able to determine that her ankles were as well. Every part of her was stiff. She tried moving the merest amount, but it was a struggle. Her limbs were still groggy, affected by whatever they had knocked her out with. Mercy was guessing chloroform.

Without being able to see or move, she relied on her ears to gather what information she could. She could hear wind and the sound of tires rolling over pavement, so she guessed the back was open to the air. Even though the ground was pavement, it got rough in spots. It was unlikely that they were on a highway, but instead were on a less used and less maintained side road. Close by, somebody cleared his throat. Mercy wasn't alone in the truck bed, but she had no idea how many were near her or their exact location. She tried to listen for other sounds of life, but heard none; the wind was drowning them out.

The truck turned to the right, or at least she thought the right, guessing that her head was toward the truck's cab. Mercy slid sideways, trying to let her body stay slack as if asleep. Her bad knee hit into something and she had to bite down on her lower lip to keep from screaming. There was nothing she could do about the way her body had momentarily stiffened from the pain, but no one made any indication that they had noticed. In fact, hands grabbed her from both sides and roughly shoved her back into place between them. So, there were at least two men in the back with her.

There was the cat, the rat, the rabbit, the wolf, and the bird. And the snake, she couldn't forget about the snake that the bird had mentioned. That made six men that she knew of. If only two were in the back with her, then the other four could be riding comfortably in the cab. Of course, there could be a fifth in the cab, and who knows who else could be in the back with her. She thought back to when she had inspected the pickup truck. She tried to gauge the size from memory, and decided if there were more than four men in the truck bed with her, she would have had to notice them by now because of how crowded it would be. So that made six, possibly nine. Mercy had been surprised by their numbers too many times now. Although she did her best to gauge how many there were, from now on she was always going to assume there were more.

The road suddenly got a lot rougher. All of Mercy's wounds vibrated painfully. She clenched her teeth together, hoping the bouncing would soon stop. A couple of huge bumps in rapid succession threw Mercy up off the truck's bed. One of the men grabbed hold of her shoulders and made sure she slammed painfully back down into place. The ride became smoother after that, but it didn't stop Mercy from having to take stock of all her wounds. They all sent signals to her brain, demanding her attention. That's when she realized she wasn't cold, when she probably should be.

Trying to send her focus out and away from her body and its pains, she realized there was a warm current of air flowing over her. It came from the direction of her head, and washed gently along her body. It wasn't hot, but it was pleasant compared to how cold she had been earlier. Perhaps there was a heater in the back of the pickup so that the men with her could keep warm.

Because we wouldn't want them to get cold, she thought bitterly to herself.

It was only a short time later that the truck finally ground to a stop. She listened as the doors to the cab were opened.

"Don't fucking touch me!" a man screamed at another.

"How am I supposed to help you get inside if I can't touch you?" another responded.

"Just be careful of my knee."

"I know. Christ, what, you think I'm an idiot or something? I've only had to listen to you whine about your fucking knee the whole way here."

So, one of the men was the wolf. She didn't recognize the other voice as any of the others she had heard speak.

One of the men in the back giggled. It was very likely the cat.

The tailgate was lowered, and the man to her right left the truck bed. Another man climbed up and took his place.

"How is she?" It was the bird.

Mercy felt a hand rest on her forehead through the bag. There was something tender about the touch. She didn't like it.

"I don't know. Alive."

"She's awake," the bird said matter-of-factly. He was more observant than the others.

"Oh, she's up? Then let me at her! I have some payback I need to exact!" the wolf called out, although his voice was farther away than before. It was hard to pinpoint the exact location of everyone outside the truck. The earth beneath it sounded like gravel, and all the different footsteps and scuffling made tracking the sounds difficult.

"Later." The rat was down by Mercy's feet. He suddenly grabbed hold of them and dragged her toward the open tailgate, toward himself.

Mercy wanted to fight, but her limbs were still so groggy and sore. Besides, she couldn't see, and her wrists and ankles were still bound. What could she do? Wiggle her way free and then make like an inchworm along the ground?

As she reached the end of the truck bed, she was rudely thrown up and over the rat's shoulders into something like a fireman's carry.

"Be careful," the bird told him, although his far away voice made it sound like it didn't make a difference to him whether the rat was actually careful or not.

She felt like a hunted deer that he was bringing home as a trophy. She could smell him while in that position too. He smelled of man sweat. It was different from Kenny's smell in that the rat's had more of a meaty texture to it. If Mercy had been able to find some food during the night, she would've been tempted to throw it up.

The rat started walking, carrying Mercy somewhere. With every step he took, she was bounced and shifted slightly. With every step, her knee flared up. She wanted to cry out, but bit down on her lower lip again. Her lip had been taking a pounding from her teeth that night, but she didn't want to show weakness. She didn't want to let these men know just how hurt she was.

"I'm going to eat you for breakfast," the wolf was suddenly near her head, whispering at her through the hood.

"Get him the fuck inside," the rat growled.

Mercy listened as a door was opened. The rat's footsteps sounded on wood, instead of gravel, and then Mercy's head and feet brushed lightly against something on either side. She got the sense that she had just passed through a doorway.

The quality of the sounds changed. There was less open space. Mercy was sure she was hearing the footsteps bouncing back at her off of walls. She couldn't tell how big the space was, but it didn't feel large. She was guessing it was an average space, like a house maybe. From one house of horror to the next.

The ride ended shortly after passing through a second doorway. Mercy could hear whimpering, but it wasn't coming from her. It wasn't the wolf, either; he was being moved around somewhere to the right, grunting and cursing at whoever was helping him. There was someone else here, someone else hurt or afraid. There was a loud creak of metal, and the rat lowered Mercy to the ground. She was harshly shoved sideways, her hip catching painfully on the lip of a metal panel she was being pushed onto. The creak sounded again followed by a clang. There was a metal on metal sound afterward, like a lock being thrown. Something grabbed her head from above and finally yanked the bag off, nearly taking a second chunk of her hair with it.

The sudden light hurt her eyes, despite its dimness. She squinted and blinked until she could see properly.

She was in a cage. To be precise, she was in a large dog crate. The floor was a flat sheet of metal and metal bars made up the other five sides of its box shape. The bars were spaced widely enough to allow an arm through, which was how they yanked her hood off, but not to allow an average-sized head through. One side was pressed up against a plaster wall while the opposite held the door to the cage. A heavy lock hung from the door.

The cage was in a room, within a house. It looked like it had once been a living room, but the place was old. The walls were broken with cracked plaster that had never been painted, scraps of faded wallpaper still clinging in places and obscene images painted in old spray paint. The ceiling was no better. The floor was warped hardwood. Dirt and dust clung to every nook and corner. The whole room was lit by a single floor lamp in one corner that had no shade, just a bare bulb.

A ratty, faded couch that was once either red or brown lay against the wall to Mercy's right, with the lamp against the far end of it. Two windows were set into the wall, but they were boarded up. To Mercy's left, along the same wall as her cage, was a second cage. Beyond that, the left side wall had two entranceways matching the locations of the windows opposite. The entranceway Mercy could see through led into a hallway, which matched the state of the living room but had a different shade of faded wallpaper. She couldn't see through the far entranceway, but suspected that it led to the front door. On the far wall hung a large painting—it was covered in cobwebs, but appeared to be of a ship in a stormy sea. Two chairs that matched the couch sat beneath it.

The wolf was lying on the couch, his head toward Mercy so that the armrest hid it from sight. His mask was lying on the floor next to him, and the belt and clothes he had grabbed from Mercy's basement were still wrapped around his leg. The rat stood next to the couch, between Mercy and the wolf, looking down at her through the barred ceiling of the cage. His mask was propped up on his forehead, which was wide and flat. His whole face had a wide and flat look, as if he had run into walls a few too many times as a child. The cat sat in one of the far chairs, his mask still on, a grin pulling on his lower face, and his eyes shining they darted from Mercy to the occupant in the other cage. The snake was sitting in the other chair, watching the wolf. His identifying mask hung from one hand by the elastic strap. His hair was close cropped and dark, and his face rough-cut. His eyes were also dark, as was his skin tone. He was a deep olive, while the rest of the men were white. It was hard to read his expression but Mercy thought he was concerned for the wolf. The bird and the rabbit were missing.

Having completely taken in all the threats she could, Mercy finally focused on the occupant in the other cage.

"Ella?" It was someone she knew. In fact, it was one of her co-workers.

"Shut up." The rat struck her cage with a piece of metal pipe that he had held behind him, making the whole thing clatter and clang. The threat in his voice was obvious.

Mercy glared up at him, trying to give him the meanest look possible, but she got the point. She wasn't going to try talking again, at least not right away. She turned back to Ella.

The woman was in her pink scrubs uniform. Tracks on her face from her makeup told of the tears she had been crying earlier. Her eyes looked like they might release more tears at any moment. She was looking at Mercy, throwing a frightful glance toward the men every now and again. Her face held an expression of concern that Mercy wasn't used to seeing directed at her. Usually she saw it on the faces of the families that came in to visit their coma patients. Mercy remembered her reflection in the bathroom mirror and understood why Ella was looking at her like that now.

Ella was a wonderful woman. She was a Canadian born into a Hispanic family and had a tendency to act as a mother hen over all the nurses, and even the doctors, in the coma ward. She was in her late forties and had a kind husband and three bright boys back home. Every year, her family would help organize a big barbecue for all the hospital staff. Her husband was a well-liked doctor who worked in the pathology department, and between the two of them, they knew virtually everybody there. She was a somewhat over-weight woman who was comfortable in her skin, with dark hair, dark eyes that lit up when she laughed, and a tendency to push chocolate on people despite their protests that they were dieting.

Most of that loving woman was gone, or at least hiding at the moment. Mercy saw in the cage next to her a frightened soul. Ella shivered even though the room was warm. Her eyes were wide and flat, their usual shine missing. She was curled up upon herself, trying to be as small as possible, which was the complete opposite of her open nature. Mercy felt the rage in her stomach burn brighter at these men. She hated them even more for reducing this woman to this. At least Ella didn't appear to be injured.

Mercy nodded at Ella, trying to tell her that she was okay. She wasn't, not really, but she didn't want the woman worrying about her more than need be. Because she didn't like to see her own fear reflected in another, Mercy turned away and focused on the interior of her cage. There was nothing in it but her. She checked out the rope around her wrists. They weren't tied very tightly, just well enough to keep them together. She brought her wrists to her face and began to use her teeth to tug and pull at the rope. The rat, although still watching her, said nothing. Apparently she was expected to untie herself. When the rope around her wrists was off, she set to work on the one around her ankles, grateful to be using her hands this time.

"Hand those to me," the rat grumbled, holding out his hand for the ropes.

Mercy debated whether to give them to him or not. She couldn't see an immediate use for the ropes, but that didn't mean there wouldn't be one in the future.

The rat smashed the side of the cage with the pipe again. The cage was solidly build, and didn't bend from the force, but the sudden loud sound caused Mercy to flinch reactively.

"I will use this pipe on you if you make me."

Mercy shoved an end of each rope through a gap in the cage bars. She wasn't going to just hand them to the man; she was going to make sure he had to put in some effort. It was a small accomplishment to watch him bend over and pull the rope out through the bars. If she moved fast, she might be able to claw at his eyes. The thought was tempting, but the pitiful amount of damage she was likely to cause didn't balance out what would probably happen to her afterward. Besides, with her knee feeling like it was, she doubted she could move fast.

The rabbit entered the room, the mask still covering his upper face. He was carrying a box that looked surprisingly clean in this dingy hole. He went over to the wolf and knelt down beside him, placing the box on the floor next to him.

"Aw, shit. *You're* going to patch me up? Fuck. We shouldn't have let the psycho kill that doctor. I'd rather have him do it than you."

The rabbit didn't respond, he just went about preparing the tools and supplies he needed. He laid a sterile drape on the floor on his other side and moved what he needed from the box to the drape. Mercy wondered if the rabbit actually knew what he was doing, if he had any real medical training, or if he was just basing his work on medical shows.

A loud squeaking and creaking of boards came from the hall, moving toward the living room. The rabbit, snake, and cat all suddenly shot to their feet. The rabbit kept his head down, looking at the floor, as he turned his body to face the door. The cat's toothy grin faded into a subtle, bemused smirk. All attention was on the entranceway. Even the wolf pulled himself as upright as he could get. With the added height, Mercy could see the top of his head peeking up over the armrest. His hair was matted with sweat, most likely from the pain caused by the bumpy ride to wherever they were.

As Mercy turned to look at the entranceway, a man in a wheelchair was rolled in. The bird, still masked although now wearing a long-sleeved shirt and clean jeans, was pushing it. The chair was rolled to the center of the room and then turned to face Mercy and Ella. The man in the chair assessed them both. He was an older man, with white hair and sagging skin. He appeared frail, but held himself upright as a man with strength and power. His eyes were sharp and alert as he looked over the two girls. There was a deep and twisted intelligence behind them.

He turned his head to take in the wolf.

"You underestimated her," the man in the wheelchair said to him. His voice held more power than his body. Whoever this man was, he was clearly in control of the others.

"We all did, sir," the snake said from behind him, defending the wolf.

The man in the wheelchair didn't acknowledge the snake. He continued to stare at the wolf a moment longer then turned to gaze at the women again. He focused on Mercy.

"Bravo, girl." He then addressed the two of them. "Do either of you remember who I am?"

The women looked at each other. Ella certainly didn't, by the look on her face. Should they know him? Mercy looked back at the man in the wheelchair, studying him more closely. She was afraid of what might happen if they didn't recognize him. He wasn't a friend of the family, or the family of a friend, but there was something familiar about the lines of his face. The man met her eyes, understanding that she was studying him. He blinked exceptionally slowly. When his eyes were fully closed, his name clicked on in Mercy's mind.

"Maxime Fowler."

Mercy knew that the moment she said his name, Ella would remember him as well. Mr. Fowler had been a patient in the coma ward for just under two years. No one knew how he came to be in coma. It was said that he had been picked up from a park bench, and no one had been able to awaken him. One day, he just suddenly came out of it: a miracle really. Mr. Fowler had been polite enough when he awoke, and didn't seem very concerned about what had happened. Mercy had been on shift when he woke up while Ella hadn't been, which was probably why she remembered him first. It was later during that shift that Mr. Fowler had disappeared from the coma ward. No one knew how or why, he was just gone. They had all expected him to show up dead within a few days, but he was never heard of again. Until now that was, over two years after vanishing.

Mr. Fowler smiled.

"You can always count on nurses to remember faces better than doctors. Which is why I thought you two might be more useful than Dr. Lynch was."

Mercy shuddered as she remembered the bird telling her that he had killed Dr. Lynch. Ella must not have known, because she just seemed confused and worried. Mercy wished that she and Ella could speak to one another, to trade notes about what was happening to them and bring each other up to speed.

"What do you want from us, Fowler?" Although Mercy was used to calling patients Mr., Mrs., and Ms., she didn't think this man deserved the formality.

"Please, call me Max," he said. "And what I want from you is to know where my kidney is."

"Your kidney?" Mercy frowned.

Ella looked down, lost in thought for a moment, probably sending her mind back to when Max had been a patient of theirs.

"His kidney was donated to someone," Ella spoke to the floor of her cage. "I can't remember who. In fact, I don't think we ever found out."

"Well you better think it over real carefully. I liked that kidney; I want to know where it is. I want to know who has it."

Mercy remembered now. On rare occasions, a power of attorney would sign a waver for a long-term coma patient, giving their approval for an organ donation to be made. Kidneys were the most popular organs, as the coma patient could continue to survive with only one. Max had been in exemplary health for a coma patient. He didn't need any machines to sustain him; his only problem was not waking up. Whoever his power of attorney was, must have said it was okay to donate, and after passing all the tests, he lost a kidney to save someone else from the dialysis machines.

"We weren't told where your kidney went," Mercy informed him. She actually couldn't recall if she had been told or not. She couldn't remember much about Max as a patient, just the strangeness of how he wound up in coma, and how he had disappeared afterward. If it hadn't been for the disappearance, she might not have remembered him at all.

"You know where it is," Max insisted. "One of you is going to tell me where my kidney is within the next twenty-four hours, or you're both going to die."

CHAPTER FOURTEEN

WITHOUT TURNING TO LOOK behind him, Max pointed over his shoulder at the snake.

"Take me back to my room."

All the men turned their heads to stare at the snake. Again, his expression was hard to read. Mercy wasn't sure if he was uncomfortable about the command, or honoured. The others' expressions gave nothing away.

As the bird stepped out of the way, the snake walked up and grabbed the wheelchair's handles. He pushed Max toward the entrance where he had come in.

"Remember girls: twenty-four hours. You don't want to end up like Dr. Lynch," and with that Max was gone, squeaking off down the hallway.

Mercy turned Ella, who stared back, her eyes wide. How could they possibly find out who had been the recipient of the organ donation? Maybe if they were back at the hospital and could go through records and things, there was a chance, but to sit in cages with only their memories? It seemed impossible.

The wolf yelped and cursed. Mercy turned and saw that the rabbit was kneeling next to him again, gingerly removing the clothing from around his knee. He took a pair of tough scissors and began cutting away his jeans.

"I'm going to need him to lie flat on his stomach," the rabbit said to the rat. "This couch is too short for that."

The rat gestured with his head for the bird and the cat to help. As the rabbit spread a large, clean blanket along the floor, the three men manhandled the wolf. Even though they were trying to be careful with his knee, he screamed, cursed, and cried out in pain several times. They laid him down on his stomach on the blanket. Fresh sweat was pouring out of his ghastly pale face, and it looked like he was bleeding again. The rabbit inspected the back of his knee, while the rat dragged the lamp over for better lighting. It was plugged into an extension cord, which made Mercy think that it was moved around fairly regularly. She wondered if the power to this ramshackle of a place was still on, or if a generator somewhere was running the lights.

The rabbit pointed at the cat. "Go get me the blood. We're going to need to set up a transfusion." He then pointed at the rat. "You go get the IV stand and saline. This is worse than we thought."

"Worse?" the wolf squeaked.

"You'll be fine," the rabbit assured him. There was something about the rabbit's voice that Mercy thought was familiar. It was soft, gentle, and honest. Although he seemed sure of the commands he was giving, he sounded unsure as to whether he should be giving them to these men. Either way, they obeyed and left the room.

The rabbit also left the room, but he was back in seconds, shoving a large cardboard box along the floor. Metal objects were rattling around inside. He pushed it near the wolf's head and left it there.

"You're in charge of that," the rabbit said to the bird.

The bird knelt beside the box and pulled a breathing mask out of it. He placed it over the wolf's head, then took a canister and hooked it up to the mask. Mercy couldn't see the label on the canister but assumed it was oxygen or maybe an anaesthetic.

The rat came back with an IV stand and stood it next to the box. Without being asked, he started to set up a line into the wolf's arm. He worked confidently, as if he had done this before. The rabbit pulled on a surgical mask over his mouth and nose, his entire face save his eyes now covered, and then snapped on a pair of surgical gloves. He looked over at Mercy and met her eyes. There was something in them that she didn't understand. He then turned back to the wolf's knee and began his work.

With the men gathered around—including the cat who had returned with a disturbing amount of blood, suggesting to Mercy that these men regularly drew and stored their own blood for just such an emergency—it was hard for Mercy to see exactly what was going on. She didn't think she needed to, however. From what she *could* see, they appeared to be operating on the wolf's knee, although in a grossly unsterile environment and in the most painful way. They weren't able to knock the wolf out, and despite whatever numbing agents and painkillers they had given him, he could still feel things. He screamed into the oxygen mask several times. Mercy thought that those must have been the times they touched a nerve.

Mercy was fairly sure she knew how much damage she had caused. Judging by the amount of blood, she had gotten a few veins, but missed the artery. He would be dead by now if she had cut his artery. His nerve had been sliced, maybe even cut through, which was the source of most of the pain. She couldn't tell exactly how much damage was done there, since she couldn't see his foot, and no one had asked about it in her presence. Outside of the nerve damage, ligaments would be the worst. Mercy felt certain that she had severed his MCL. Although she could be wrong, she didn't think she was. It would be a long time before the wolf could walk again; *if* he ever walked again that was. It depended on just how much damage Mercy had managed and how good the rabbit was at knee surgery. At best, he'd probably have a permanent limp.

Through most of the surgery, the wolf's eyes bored into Mercy. They glared and burned into her from over his oxygen mask. The only times he looked away was when the pain became so excruciating that his eyes rolled wildly. Even when the bird was between them to change the small oxygen canister to a new one, Mercy could feel the hate radiating off of him. She got the feeling that if she didn't come up with something to tell Max in twenty-four hours, it would be the wolf that killed her. And he would take great pleasure in doing it slowly.

It was impossible for Mercy to tell how long the surgery lasted, but eventually the rabbit backed away and stripped off his bloodied surgical gloves. The wolf was on his back now; his knee wrapped in a clean white bandage and locked up in a brace. The cat and rat helped him up unto his good leg and assisted him in hobbling out of the room. It sounded like they were going up a staircase to someplace, probably to a bedroom where he could rest. After taking off his surgical mask, the rabbit picked up his box of supplies and carried them over to Mercy's cage. Mercy quickly pushed herself to the back of it.

"I'm just going to take a look at your knee," the rabbit told her.

"Actually, I thought I would do that," the bird said, striding over. He had pushed his bird mask up onto his head during the surgery, revealing a face made of sharp, thin angles. Mercy thought she could probably cut herself on cheekbones like those.

The rabbit looked from Mercy to the bird, unsure of what to do. He clearly didn't want to oppose the bird. Mercy, though, wanted him to. She didn't want the bird touching her.

The snake suddenly appeared in the room, facing the bird. "Max wants you."

The bird nodded. He looked down at Mercy. "Maybe next time." He then left the room. Having him out of sight lifted a weight off Mercy that she hadn't been aware she was carrying.

The snake turned to the rabbit. "Where's...?" He let the question hang, perhaps deliberately avoiding giving him a name or moniker.

"They should be getting him situated upstairs," the rabbit told him.

The snake nodded and also left the room. The old and hollow house made him easy to track as he climbed the steps and went to a room at, what Mercy assumed, was the opposite corner of the house.

She and Ella were now alone with the rabbit.

"Can I take a look at your leg?" he asked.

Mercy thought about it. She couldn't see the harm in just letting him look. Besides, maybe he could lessen the pain, which would do nothing but help Mercy. She slowly scooted over to the edge of the cage and untied the sweater from around her knee. The pajama pants were crusted to the skin with dried blood. The rabbit reached into his box and took out a bottle of clean saline and some gauze pads.

"May I?" he asked, gesturing from the bottle to her knee.

She nodded. The rabbit put his arms through the bars, saline in one hand, gauze pads in the other. Mercy could've grabbed those arms and pulled, smashing his face into the bars, but again, what would be the use? She had no way of getting out of the cage and the box of medical supplies was too far to reach. She also had the impression that the rabbit wasn't the kind of man who would be given a key to the cage. The rat probably had it.

The rabbit gently poured some saline over Mercy's knee and dabbed at it with the gauze. It hurt some, and Mercy sucked in a sharp breath through her teeth. He ignored her pain as he cleaned the wound.

"It looks like there's no major damage," the rabbit reported, "but it should be stitched up."

He looked up into Mercy's eyes, waiting for her to tell him if he should do that or not. Mercy nodded.

As he numbed up the area and prepared the needle and thread, Mercy again thought about hurting the man. She wondered if she could pick the lock with the needle. Probably not. At least not before one of the other men returned.

Wincing, Mercy watched as her knee was closed up. The numbing agents felt good, providing sweet relief. When he was done, the rabbit wrapped her knee in a loose bandage and handed her a couple of antibiotics through the bars. She popped the pills and dry swallowed them, not realizing that that could have been a bad idea until after they hit her stomach. The rabbit could have just handed her hallucinogens or cyanide for all she knew. Too late for that now, she would just have to hope that he had handed her what she had assumed.

"Do you have any other bad injuries?" the rabbit asked.

"My feet," Mercy admitted.

"Let me see."

She stripped out of her shoes and socks and let the rabbit clean and inspect her feet.

"Did you go through formal medical training?" Mercy asked, watching as he placed bandages over the worst spots. She had noticed that his stitches were impeccable.

The rabbit didn't answer.

"You must have had some training," Mercy continued. Anything she could learn about these men was to her advantage. "There's no way you could figure out how to do all this from just books. How much practice have you had patching people up?"

Still silence. When he finished, he packed everything back into his box and rose to his feet with it.

"Someone will come by later with some food." He walked out of the room, leaving Ella and Mercy alone in their cages. The women immediately drew together.

"Are you okay?" they asked at the exact same time.

"Where did they grab you?" Mercy quickly followed up before Ella could ask something else.

"As I was leaving work," Ella told her. "I was heading to my car in the parking garage, and then all of a sudden this bag was thrown over my head. I kicked and screamed but they held something over my mouth. I think it was chloroform. Next thing I knew I woke up in this cage, and those men were standing around. I tried to talk to them but they either ignored me or threatened to hurt me. Then they all left. I think several hours went by, I'm not sure, I may have fallen asleep, and then you arrived. What happened to you?"

"They attacked me at my parents' house. I tried to fight them off but clearly I didn't succeed in the end. I think you're right about the chloroform. They used it on me too."

"Are your parents okay?" Ella had met them a few times. Mercy's dad tried to attend all the fundraisers.

"Yeah, they were out of the house. Bit of a family emergency happened, but that's all okay now." Mercy didn't want to get into the details about baby Robin. It didn't seem right to even think about him in a place like this.

"I hope my family is okay," Ella worried.

"You said they grabbed you from the parking garage, right? I'm sure they're fine."

"Maybe. But we got some kind of threatening phone calls before I was grabbed."

"You too, huh? I've gotten a few of those since Friday. Was it the rat?"

"The who?"

"The rat. The kind of short, wide one. He wears a rat mask."

"Oh, I hadn't noticed it was a rat. But no, I don't think it was him. He has a deep voice doesn't he?"

"Yeah, and really smooth-sounding."

"No. If I had to guess, I would think it was that darker skinned man who called us."

"The snake." Mercy remembered something the bird had said, wondering if it was the rat or the snake that had gone after her in the house. The way he spoke made it sound like the choice was based on who had called her, and if two people had made calls, it stood to reason that two different men may have gone in after her.

"I guess."

"So you don't really know anything about them?" Mercy was disappointed.

"No. Do you?"

"Not really. I think there's six of them, and Max. Although there could be more I haven't seen yet. They have guns, or at least the cat was carrying around a shotgun earlier, and the rabbit had a pistol. I was shot at but they missed."

Ella's eyes widened at the tale.

"They work together fairly well, but I don't think they get along perfectly. There seems to be some sort of hierarchy among them. I think the rat is near the top, and the rabbit is at the bottom. I haven't figured out the rest yet. The bird is the worst. He-" Mercy cut herself off, not knowing whether she should tell Ella about the Abrams or even what she knew about Dr. Lynch.

"What?" Ella pressed, aching for information.

"He killed my parents' neighbours. And he told me he killed Dr. Lynch."

Ella gasped, clamping both her hands over her mouth. A single tear escaped her right eye, tried to follow the path of those before it, and got stopped by the side of her hand.

"So do you have any idea about who Max's kidney could have gone to?" Mercy didn't try to be subtle at all with her topic change.

Ella seemed confused for a moment, still distracted and distraught over the news that Mercy had just given her. She lowered her hands from her face, her eyes darting about the cage as if the answer were pinned to the bars.

"Uhhh," she stalled, trying to form thoughts. "No. I don't really remember Max that much. Just that he disappeared. I would never have remembered his name if you hadn't said it first. Lynch is really dead?"

"Damn. I can't remember anything either. I remember how he showed up at the hospital, and how he disappeared, but I can't remember anything in-between. Especially, not a kidney transfer." She deliberately avoided mentioning Lynch. She didn't want the conversation to veer off topic. She probably shouldn't have told her what happened in the first place, but it would at least let Ella know that these men were serious about their threats.

Footsteps echoed down the stairs. Both women fell silent. They watched as the rat walked past the entranceway near them, only glancing in at them as he passed by. He continued down the hall, to where Mercy didn't know.

"Tell me exactly what you remember about Max," Mercy whispered in case the rat wasn't far off. "Maybe it'll help some memories come back."

"Umm." Ella looked around her cage again. It was as if she thought herself asleep and needed to keep checking that the bars were indeed still there. "When was it?"

"It was about two years ago. He woke up May the 16th." Mercy always remembered the dates of when patients woke up. She wasn't always the best with remembering names or faces, but voices and dates she was good with.

"Two years ago…" Ella nervously tugged on a lock of her hair that hung next to her face. "I remember. Thomas was nearing the end of grade six, and he was terrified about having to start at a new school for grade seven." Thomas was her middle son. "I wasn't on shift. I didn't even know Max had woken up until I went in the next day and heard about it and his disappearance. How did he end up in coma?"

"Nobody ever found out. He was found on a park bench and brought in to us. Everyone looked him over but nobody ever found anything wrong. If I remember right, he was our healthiest patient while with us. He never had any breathing or heart troubles."

Ella nodded. "Yes, I can remember that now. We had him for a year, right? Never a problem with him. Wasn't even prone to bed sores."

"A year and eight months." It probably wasn't necessary to mention the eight months, but that did put it closer to two years, which might get Ella focusing on a broader scope of memories.

Ella tugged on the same lock of her hair again. It was a nervous gesture that Mercy had never seen her do before. A part of her was curious as to whether it was a new tic, or an old childhood habit returning.

Something itched at the back of Mercy's mind. There was an idea back there, not fully formed, but she was sure it had an answer for her. Before she could focus on getting it out, footsteps came toward the living room again.

Mercy and Ella turned toward the entranceway and watched as the rat returned. He had two bottles of water with him and a plate full of sandwiches. He dropped a bottle of water through the top of each cage, Mercy's hitting off her shoulder before bouncing and rolling along the bottom. The rat placed the plate on the floor between the two cages and left the room again without saying a word.

The sandwiches were just baloney and margarine on white bread. Mercy's stomach roared from the smell. She reached through the bars and picked up one of the sandwiches. Ella grabbed one from the other side, their hands both able to reach the plate, but came just an inch short of being able to reach each other.

With her hunger in full control, Mercy wolfed down the sandwich. She didn't like baloney. The taste didn't appeal to her, and she was grossed out by the slimy texture, but at that moment she didn't care. When one was done, she grabbed the next. Ella ate her own sandwich more slowly, watching as Mercy finished her second and grabbed the last sandwich on the plate.

Mercy was about to bite into her third sandwich when she noticed Ella watching her. She looked down and saw that she had grabbed three to Ella's one.

"Do you want the last one?" Mercy offered, holding the sandwich out.

"No." Ella shook her head and tried to smile. "You're clearly much hungrier than I am."

Mercy didn't bother to ask again and resumed eating. With every bite she took, she got more and more tired. Her head began to droop, and her eyes kept drifting closed. For a moment she snapped awake, thinking that the food was drugged, but she was pretty sure that that wasn't it. Her body had just run out of adrenaline and had reached the limit of how long it could stay awake.

"You're exhausted," Ella commented. "Why don't you close your eyes and sleep for a bit?"

"No." Mercy shook her head and finished her sandwich. She cracked open the water bottle and washed the food down with a large swig. "We need to figure out what we're going to do."

"You can't keep going like this. Maybe if you get some rest your mind will run better. I took a nap earlier, I'm not tired. You sleep. I'll keep an eye out if any of those men come back."

Mercy's head lolled on her neck. Her eyes kept closing for longer and longer periods. She was going to fall asleep soon, whether she liked it or not.

"Okay. Just wake me up if anything happens. And I mean anything."

Ella nodded.

Mercy closed her eyes and lay down on her side, using her arms and sweater as a pillow. There wasn't enough room to stretch out, the floor was hard, her body ached, and the light was too bright. Still, her exhaustion finally managed to claim her.

CHAPTER FIFTEEN

Mercy didn't make it into a deep sleep; she dreamt the entire time.

In her dream, she was back at the hospital. She wandered through the empty halls, looking for someone or something. She went to the coma ward, and there she saw Max, lying in his patient's bed. He was awake though, and started screaming at Mercy. He was demanding that she find his legs, which was silly, because they were attached to him. Still, she searched about the ward. She searched and searched while Max continued to shout at her. The hospital was decaying, and the longer things went on, the more ruinous it became. Windows cracked and fell out, cupboard doors separated from their hinges, empty beds became moldy, even the floor split, and a large tree began growing through it. Still Mercy searched and searched, becoming increasingly frantic.

She was partly awakened when her injured knee rubbed against her other leg. She was then brought to full wakefulness by the sounds of gentle weeping. Mercy dragged her eyelids open and checked on Ella. The woman was sitting in one of the corners of her cage, crying into her hands.

"Ella?" Mercy's voice came out frog-like.

Ella startled and sat up straighter, wiping her hands quickly over her eyes. "I'm sorry. Did I wake you?"

"No," Mercy half lied as she pulled herself upright. She thought about asking Ella what was wrong, but she knew. She was worried about never seeing her children again. Mercy just didn't have the energy to ask and go through the conversation that would follow. It would only end with her giving Ella false promises about getting out of there.

She located her water bottle and took a drink. The plate was still present, and still empty. The house was quiet.

"How long have I been out?" she wondered.

"A few hours, I think," Ella told her. The woman looked like she was aching to be asked about the crying. Still, Mercy couldn't bring herself to start the conversation.

"Have you heard anything from the men? Have they moved around at all?"

"No."

"I bet they're sleeping." Mercy figured that now would be the best time to see about escape. She maneuvered herself to the front of the cage and reached her arms through the bars. Grabbing the lock, she pulled it into a position that allowed her to get a good look at it. It was not the kind of lock she was expecting. Instead of a keyhole, which she could attempt to pick open with the right item, it was a combination lock. It was made so that you'd have to twist a set of four number wheels into the right positions to open it. Mercy tugged on the chunk of metal, but it obviously wasn't open. Four zeroes was not the combo.

Mercy got angry at the lock. She clawed at it, pulling, twisting the dials into random configurations. It stood between her and her freedom. Mercy rounded on the bars next. She grabbed at them, tried to pry them apart, tried to fit her head through. She had read somewhere that if you could fit your head through something, you should be able to get the rest of your body through by contorting it. The head though was key, as the solid mass of bone couldn't be bent, twisted, or squeezed. It was no good; none of the gaps were large enough.

Ella was cowering in her corner, watching Mercy, not helping their predicament at all.

"Have you checked your lock yet?" Mercy asked, more snappishly than she had intended.

Ella shook her head.

"Well, go on then." She gestured to the front of Ella's cage with her arm. "And check all the bars, see if any of them are weaker than the others."

While Ella timidly moved to the front of her cage, Mercy started investigating the corners of her own. She had a slightly similar cage at home from the time she and Kenny had adopted Roofus. The crate he had been trained in was smaller than this one, but more importantly, was designed to be easily taken apart for storage. It was possible that this cage was made the same way, and if so, it might be possible to take it apart from the inside.

Mercy quickly found out that this was not the case. Although it seemed like it could have been possible at one time, all the hinges, clips, and bolts had been soldered together. Some even had new pieces of metal welded on top for extra security. There was no way Mercy could take it apart.

As Mercy's options whittled away to nothing, she started to panic. Her rational mind faded into the background as she started to come up with more and more irrational ideas. She kept crawling around the cage, unable to stand, being less mindful of her injured knee than she should have been. She started shaking the bars, pulling at them, trying to pry them apart. She lashed out at her confinement, screaming, throwing her shoulder at the sides, causing the cage to shift small amounts. She even clawed at the back wall, pulling off useless chunks of water-damaged plaster. Ella was terrified in the next cage over, curled up and crying again. Mercy ended up lying on her back, kicking the cage door with her good leg over and over again.

When the bird walked into the room she didn't even notice. She didn't notice until he moved swiftly into her field of view, reached through the bars with lightning-quick reflexes, and grabbed her foot in an iron grip.

"You woke him up. He's assuming it's not because you know where his kidney is." The bird's odd voice wasn't as neutral or gentle as it previously had been. "He needs his rest, and I assure you that he will get it. Do we have an understanding?"

Mercy nodded. The bird let go of her shoe, letting her leg drop to the cage floor with a final clang. He turned toward Ella.

"Please try not to cry so loudly. It irritates him almost as much as her rattling."

Ella sniffled loudly, her breath hitching in her chest as she tried to calm down. From inside his long sleeve, a sharp scalpel slid out into the bird's hand as if by magic. He moved closer to Ella and showed her the blade.

"Mercy here has already seen an example of what I can do. You haven't. You wouldn't want her to have to see another example, would you?"

Ella clamped her hands over her mouth and furiously shook her head with enough force to throw a tear or two off her cheeks. The corners of the bird's mouth twitched as if to smile. He rose to his feet.

"He'll tolerate talking so long as it's about finding out where his kidney is, but nothing else." The bird's lithe form moved towards the entranceway, his scalpel disappearing up his sleeve again. The cat was waiting there. "Watch them. Don't make him send me out again."

The cat smiled, although it wasn't as broad or as insanely earnest as usual. This was a fake smile. The bird disappeared down the hall, and the cat sauntered into the room. When he looked at the women in their cages, his smile became a real one. He took a seat across the room.

Mercy noticed that the cat was still wearing his mask despite having stripped out of his hooded sweatshirt. She got the impression that this guy didn't just wear the mask to hide his identity, but that he enjoyed it. He liked peering out at the world through two holes cut into a piece of shaped rubber. While Mercy and the cat watched each other, he took out a cigarette and lit it.

There was something about the bird's visit that was bothering Mercy. The threats obviously bothered her, they absolutely scared her, but there was something else about it. Something else that had to do with

Max being their patient. It was right on the tip of her brain but refused to go over the edge and reveal itself.

Mercy tried and tried to think of where Max's kidney could have gone, but she just had no idea. She couldn't even remember his surgery, and whether it had been one she had scrubbed in on. She didn't think it was. Although she could picture Max lying there under the surgical lights, it could easily just be her imagination filling in the gaps of a real memory.

She wracked her brain while the cat smoked his way through two cigarettes and one joint. The smell of tobacco and marijuana permeated the air. In the cage next to Mercy's, Ella appeared to be sleeping.

"Has anyone fed them breakfast yet?" a voice spoke from the entranceway nearest the cat. Mercy couldn't see who it was, and he spoke so quietly that she wouldn't even have heard him had the house not been so silent.

"Don't think so."

"I'll do it."

"No, no." The cat rose to his feet. "I'll do it. I got the munchies anyway. You watch them."

The cat got up and walked toward the cages. Mercy watched him approach, exuding as much hate from her eyes as possible. The cat just smiled at her. He always had this look as if he knew something that Mercy didn't. She wouldn't be surprised if he did, but she just wished she could wipe the smug, condescending look off his face.

"I have to pee," Mercy said to the cat, although she didn't actually have to go since she'd relieved herself in the river.

"Then pee. I'm not stopping you." Apparently they weren't going to open the cages for any reason.

He grabbed the plate off the floor between the cages. Ella stirred a little but didn't waken. She was hiding in her dreams, something that Mercy had wanted to do last night, while the men were after her, but she had convinced herself that it would have been suicide. The cat glanced back at the entranceway and waited for whoever he had been talking to to enter. It was the rabbit. When the rabbit took a seat across the room, the cat walked out.

Whereas the cat had spent his time staring directly at Mercy and Ella, the rabbit looked everywhere but. He was clearly uncomfortable being alone in the room with the two women. He still wore his mask, but unlike the cat, Mercy didn't get the impression that he wore it because he liked it. He scratched the skin under the edges of it a few times, and readjusted it a lot. Mercy thought that maybe he wore it because he didn't want her to see his face.

A stone weighted down Mercy's gut. She had just come to realize something. All the other men in the house had taken their masks off as if it were no big deal if the women saw their faces. They obviously didn't expect the women to leave here alive. Even if she could come up with the location of Max's kidney, she was a dead woman. She had been wasting her time clawing through her memories, when escape was her only option.

The rabbit shifted uncomfortably. So if the others didn't think Mercy or Ella would leave this place, then why was the rabbit still wearing his mask? Was it possible that he was worried Mercy or Ella might still escape? It didn't seem likely. Although he didn't come across as being nearly as confident as the others, he must know how slim the odds were. And besides, it seemed like the kind of thing for which the other men would make fun of him. Whatever his reason, Mercy didn't believe he was hiding his identity in case she got out and gave his description to the cops. The only other reason she could think of, was that she already knew him.

The idea struck home. What if she knew this man? Wouldn't that make sense? How they had found out where she lived, her phone numbers, all of it? Of course, they could have just followed her and looked up her number in the phone book. They may have even broken into her apartment while she out, rifled through her things, found her cell phone number, the address of her parents' house. They probably listened to the message her mom had recorded, the one about the changed time for their dinner plans. They seemed to know exactly where she was going to be on Sunday.

What if Robin's accident, wasn't an accident?

No, that was too absurd. There was no way they could've known how Mercy would've reacted to that news. They couldn't possibly know that Mercy would stay at her parents' place, instead of rushing to the hospital. That truly was just an accident; one that may have saved the rest of her family's lives, Mercy came to realize. If they hadn't been out, the men may have come anyway, and killed the Chalmers just like they had needlessly killed the Abrams.

They knew that Mercy hadn't called the cops. Was it possible that the rabbit was a cop? That could be how they got the police scanner. Maybe she knew him through Kenny somehow. Her mind felt like it was on fire as she thought through all the police officers she had met. Only one fit the rabbit's height, weight, and the way he held himself, but it couldn't be him because the ears were all wrong. Kenny's cop friend had big ears that stuck out at the sides while the rabbit's did not.

Where did she know him from then?

The rabbit shifted uncomfortably. He knew that Mercy was staring at him, evaluating him. Did he know that she was trying to place him? Maybe, it was hard to say for sure.

He couldn't be a cop. The way that he had stitched up Mercy's knee suggested medical training. Was it possible he was a doctor? He couldn't be someone who Mercy worked with or she would have recognized him right away. Someone she passed in the halls perhaps? Her mind rolled back through a rolodex of faces, bodies, and postures. She couldn't place him in scrubs or a white coat. She couldn't imagine him being at the hospital socials either.

The rabbit had become fidgety. He ran both his hands over his ears; trying and failing to tuck his slightly too long hair behind them. She had seen the gesture before. He then hunched over and began to tap his front teeth with his thumbnail. At a glance, it would appear that he was picking his teeth or lips or maybe biting the nail, but in fact, he was just bouncing his thumbnail off his hard tooth.

At last the thought that had been bugging Mercy, came to light.

For Max's kidney to have been donated, he needed a power of attorney to sign off on all the paperwork. Max had only ever had one visitor, who came just once a month, if that: his son.

"Reedus Fowler." Mercy had finally recalled the man's name. She could picture him perfectly now, sitting at Max's bedside, staring at his face, fidgeting nervously. Mercy remembered commenting on the tooth/thumbnail habit to another nurse. She also remembered that he was the one who had identified Max for them.

The rabbit, or rather Reedus, shot up to his feet, his eyes so wide they nearly filled the holes in his mask. His gaze had locked on Mercy, and then shot to the entranceway near her. The cat was there, holding a plate of sandwiches. He wasn't smiling anymore.

CHAPTER SIXTEEN

"How does she know your name?" the cat demanded. The calm demeanor he had been drifting around in was completely gone.

Reedus didn't move or speak. Mercy couldn't understand why. He just had to tell him about seeing each other at the hospital.

"How does she know your fucking name?!" the cat screeched. He threw the plate to the ground, the glass shattering into hundreds of pieces that skittered off across the floor. Sandwich bread and toppings splattered and bounced on the hardwood.

Ella woke up with a startled *yipe!* like that of a small dog, and Reedus flinched. Still, he didn't move or speak.

"I saw him at the hospital," Mercy spoke up, unsure if it was the right thing to do or not.

"You were at the hospital?" the cat growled at Reedus.

"I just wanted to see that he was being well taken care of." Reedus's voice came out small. He seemed ashamed of himself.

"We all agreed not to go there!"

Mercy noticed one of the plate shards, a large one, lying near the edge of her cage. Neither the cat nor Reedus were paying attention to her. She grabbed the shard and hid it within her bundled sweater.

Reedus was silent, staring down at his feet. Light suddenly dawned on the cat's face; he had thought of something.

"It was you! You were the one that signed the forms! It's because of you that dad's kidney is gone!"

All the colour drained away from the part of Reedus's face that Mercy could see. He suddenly bolted. He ran from the room, exiting by the entranceway near him. The cat ran after him. The door to the front of the house was opened as both men took off, one chasing after the other with malice in his eyes.

The whole house was suddenly alive.

Upstairs, the wolf was cursing and roaring. It was impossible to tell whether it was because of pain in his knee, his inability to get out of bed, or the things the cat had shouted. The pounding of feet echoed throughout the house as the two mobile men upstairs crashed their way toward the steps. The snake must have flown out the front door while the rat ran in to check on the girls. The bird appeared moments later, pushing Max in his wheelchair.

"What's going on?!" Max shouted, completely enraged. He looked at Mercy and Ella.

Mercy was sitting up against the door of her cage, her sweater hiding the plate shard on her lap. Ella was the opposite, crunched up against the wall and hiding her head in her arms.

"I remembered that the man wearing the rabbit mask is your son, Reedus. He came to see you at the hospital, and was your power of attorney. He's the one that gave the hospital permission to take your kidney." Mercy couldn't see any point in lying or holding anything back.

The rat's face twisted into an expression of revulsion and anger.

"Go get them," Max ordered the rat.

The rat turned and headed for the door.

"Make sure to bring Reedus back alive!" Max called after him as he left the house.

It was now just Max, Mercy, Ella, and the bird. Max looked at the two imprisoned women.

"You did well, Mercy," he said to her. "I had always been wondering who had signed that order but we were never able to get a copy. Perhaps now we'll be able to get some more useful information."

"What are you going to do with me?" she asked. She didn't realize that she had only asked about herself and not about Ella.

"I'm not sure yet. I see potential in you."

"Potential?" Mercy frowned.

Max looked at the bird. "Get her out of there."

The bird walked up to Mercy's cage and knelt down. Now was her chance. She watched him turn the dials to the correct numbers. She watched him pull open the lock. She watched him take off the lock, and open the latch. She watched him start to pull the door open.

Mercy sprang at the door, shoving it into the bird as hard as she could. At the same moment, she pulled out her plate shard and sliced it across the side of the bird's leg. He toppled to the ground, as she flew to her feet. The injury she had caused the bird wasn't serious, and with her bad knee, Mercy knew she couldn't out-run him. Instead she flew at Max, who raised his arms in defense. She grabbed one of those arms and yanked Max up, wheeling him around and holding him in front of her as a human shield.

Max was light, all skin and bones. His legs paddled uselessly at the floor. Although he could still move them, they were terribly weak and atrophied. No doubt it was these men who had taken Max from the hospital the day he had woken up. They knew nothing about rehabilitation after a prolonged coma, and so Max hadn't improved as well as he should have since being asleep. Mercy held the point of the plate shard to his neck.

The bird was already back on his feet. He was looking at Mercy with constantly changing expressions. She saw pain, fear, joy, remorse, anger, hope, and horrible combinations of them as well as others she couldn't identify.

"Open Ella's cage!" Mercy demanded.

The bird didn't move.

"Open it!" She pressed the point against Max's neck, even managing to shake loose a small squawk from him.

"Do it," Max told the bird.

The bird turned toward Ella's cage. Ella cringed even farther into the corner. He undid the lock, opened the latch, and let the door swing open. He stepped away from the cage, his bleeding leg not even seeming to register. Ella didn't move.

"Ella!" Mercy screamed at her. "Get your ass out of that cage! Now!"

Ella squeaked and crawled out. She hurried over to Mercy and hid behind her, her nervous hands clutching and tugging at the back of her shirt. Keeping her eyes on the bird, Mercy began to walk backward, shoving Ella forward and dragging Max along with her. The bird took a step to follow.

"No!" Mercy yelled at him. "You're going to stay right there until I'm out of here!"

The bird stopped and stood where he was. His body took on the same posture and his face the same expression as when Mercy had first met him in the Abram house. Mercy backed out of the living room.

The hallway led through the center of the house. One half held the staircase, somewhere at the top of which the wolf was still howling with rage. The far end looked like it terminated in the kitchen, and a door to one side was probably Max's room. The door behind her was the only one that mattered though: the one that led outside.

Max started laughing as they neared the door.

"Shut up." Mercy shook him.

He started laughing harder, practically hysterical. "If you ever get bored with your life, dearie, look me up."

"Ella, open the door," Mercy ordered.

Ella fumbled with the doorknob, rattling it excessively before finally getting it open. When at last she had it, Mercy felt sunlight fall upon her back. She shoved Max to the ground, still laughing, and turned toward the fresh air.

As the sun rose, Mercy pushed Ella out ahead of her, and stumbled into the light, free again, but still nowhere near safe.

CHAPTER SEVENTEEN

The air had never been fresher, even though it smelled like a swamp. The sun had never felt warmer, despite the cold breeze coming off the lake. Mercy had never been so awake, despite her lack of sleep and the excessive amounts of energy she had been putting out lately. She took in her surroundings at a glance.

To the left, which was also the east where the sun was, the ground sloped down a very weedy, patchy lawn. At the end of it was a large, circular lake. The lake itself seemed to have gone stagnant, with greenish algae floating in clumps all over the surface. Across the lake other houses could be seen, all of them run down and abandoned. Battered, twisted, and broken docks jutted out over the water along the entire shoreline like rotten teeth. Forest surrounded the houses, and had filled in the spaces between them, including the one from which Mercy and Ella had just escaped. The pickup truck sat on a gravel drive in front of the house, the early light revealing it to be dark blue. The gravel drive itself cut through more patchy grass to the right and then disappeared into the woods.

Mercy knew that the truck didn't have keys in it, otherwise Reedus would have taken off in the vehicle. She also figured that Reedus would have run straight away from the house, toward the nearest trees. At least, that's what Mercy would have done if the cat were hot on her heels. She decided to go around the house, head for the forest behind it.

As Mercy turned to run, she grabbed Ella's wrist and tried to pull her along. Ella resisted.

"No, we can take the truck," she insisted, finally showing some spine, however bad her timing was. "We can take the truck and get out of here!"

"There's no keys!" Mercy pulled again, but Ella dug her feet in.

"No!" She yanked her arm loose from Mercy's grasp, perhaps not believing her, or just not wanting to. She ran for the truck.

Fuck her, Mercy thought as she ran toward the patchy, sloping lawn. She bolted around the side of the house, past the boarded-up windows of the living room. Through the walls she could hear the wolf cursing. He was certainly an angry one. She continued on past the end of the house, and with a few more strides, she among the trees. It was a lot easier to run through the woods with her shoes on, even with her throbbing injuries.

The numbing agent that Reedus had used on her knee hadn't lasted long. Adrenaline had kept the pain at bay during her escape, but she didn't get far into the trees before it came back with a vengeance. It slowed her down to a quick hobble. There was also the risk of tearing open the stitches.

Mercy popped out of the dense brush onto another weed-choked lawn. Another house stood in front of her: this one with a stone wall leading all the way up into a chimney. No windows faced the woods she had come out of. Needing a place to rest and evaluate her knee, Mercy went around the side of the building. She came across some boarded windows but she couldn't pry the wood off them. A door was next, but the thick wooden planks hammered across it were even more solid. Just as she was thinking of moving on, she spotted bright red spray paint forming a circle under one of the windows. Mercy went over to it and peered through the gaps in the boards. The room was emptier and dirtier than the one she had fled, but there was more spray paint adorning the walls inside, as well as beer and liquor bottles scattered about. Clearly some kids had been able to get in. Mercy pressed on the boards and found that the bottom ones easily fell away.

Once the boards were knocked down—making a noise that Mercy was uncomfortable with—there was a hole just large enough for her to fit through. She squeezed her way in and landed amongst the debris below. Quickly, she righted herself, turned around, and propped the boards back up. They rested on a pair of large nails sticking out of the wall, no doubt put there by partying teens.

The light within the house was dim. Sun peeped through gaps in the wood over windows, casting beams in an almost church-like way, patterning the floor and walls. Once her eyes adjusted, she moved deeper into the house, taking care to avoid the mess. Even though it seemed the kids had set up this place to be returned to, and perhaps even had on several occasions, Mercy got the impression that no one had been here in a long time.

Mercy wandered the dark building until she found a door she could push her way through. A small room lay beyond the door, with the world's dirtiest mattress filling up most of the floor space. This was the love shack section of the party house. Needing to rest her knee, Mercy hobbled over and sat on the corner of the mattress, placing as little of her on it as she could. She sighed with relief once the pressure was off her leg.

With the door closed behind her, Mercy felt somewhat safer. She didn't trust that sense of security however. She probably wouldn't feel completely safe or secure ever again.

In her hand she still held the glass shard with the end wrapped up in her sweater. At least she had a weapon this time. For now, she laid it on the mattress next to her so that she could take a look at her knee. With her pants rolled up, she gently pulled the bandage back. Some blood had oozed out between the stitches, but not enough to cause any concern. More importantly, she hadn't popped any of the stitches. Reedus had done a fine job.

As she inspected her other wounds and rested her leg, Mercy thought about where she might be. The lake and houses made her think she was in cottage country somewhere. Perhaps the houses had been abandoned when the lake had turned and gone funky. Mercy had woken up on the way there, while Ella said she had woken up in the cage. If the same thing had been used to knock them out, then maybe Ella had been grabbed from a closer location. So if the hospital in the city was closer than her parents' place, then maybe she was in the woods on the other end of the city? To the west?

Crash.

The boards over the window had fallen to the floor. Mercy instantly shot to her feet, on the alert. It was possible that the boards had just fallen over on their own, but she didn't think so. She was certain that she had placed them back on the nails correctly. Her ears strained to hear something more.

Silence.

Mercy quickly fixed the bandages back over her knee and grabbed her glass shard. Being extra careful to make no sound, she moved over to the wall space behind the door. She wasn't taking any chances.

Clink, click, clink.

Someone had entered the house and hadn't avoided the bottles as carefully as Mercy had. And why would he? He wasn't being hunted like Mercy was. She wondered which one had come in. The rat probably, or maybe the snake.

She slowed her breathing, steeling her nerves for what she planned to do. There was no hope of staying hidden. When she had entered, there was no way to avoid leaving a trail through the dust and dirt. No, this time, she would attack. She would attack, and wouldn't just leave some flesh wound. She planned to kill.

Floorboards creaked not far from where Mercy hid. All her muscles tensed. Slowly the door swung open, hiding her behind it. She waited a moment for the man to walk into the room.

When she guessed the time was right, Mercy threw the door shut. It hit the man who had opened it, causing him to spin around, so that Mercy's plate shard was driven deep into his belly. She pressed as hard as possible, trying to reach the abdominal aorta. She was looking him in the eyes as his organs and muscles were punctured.

Only they weren't any man's eyes; they were Ella's.

Mercy gasped and backed away, letting go of the weapon. Ella stared at her, confused. She looked down at the piece of plate sticking out of her abdomen. Most of it was gone, hidden within her body, only a small, white line still protruding. It rapidly turned red. Her face twisted in pain and she fell over backward, landing squarely on the disgusting mattress. Blood poured out of her wound, adding to the filth.

She looked at Mercy, her eyes begging a thousand questions. Why did you leave me? Why did you stab me? Why were we kidnapped? Why me? Why, why, why, and most importantly, why aren't you trying to help me?

But Mercy couldn't move. Her legs had firmly taken root to the floor. Her arms were locked in the slightly bent positions they had been in when Ella fell. She could barely even blink, or breathe. Ella's own breaths were coming in the short, painful gasps of the badly injured. Mercy may not have severed the aorta, but she had probably nicked it. Ella's insides were filling with blood. Not only was the bleeding reducing the amount of oxygen that could reach Ella's brain, but it was suffocating her by squeezing her lungs.

Still Mercy couldn't move. She watched as Ella's pink scrubs stained a dark red, the mattress taking on the same colour. The room didn't smell musty anymore, like it had when Mercy first arrived, but now bore the hard, metallic scent of blood. Ella's skin was paler than Mercy had ever seen it before.

Ella was the first to look away. Her eyes drifted up toward the ceiling, seeing past the cracked and peeling plaster. If she really tried, she could have spoken, but she didn't. She just wheezed and gasped and smothered Mercy with silent guilt. Ella had a husband. She had children. She was a wonderful person who had done nothing but good.

Mercy had killed her.

Finally, she moved. Slowly at first, tentatively, but she did move. She made her way to Ella's side and bent down next to her, resting her weight on her good knee. Her own pants soaked up some of Ella's blood that had made it to the floor. She reached out to touch Ella, but stopped. Ella was gone. Her chest no longer rose and fell. Her eyes contained no inner light. She was dead.

Mercy's vision flooded with tears. Her mind went cold and blank. She had been prepared to kill one of the men, one of her captors who had tortured and terrified her, not a friend. Not a co-worker. Not a scared woman who just wanted to go home.

She rose to her feet and backed away from the lifeless body. Mercy bumped into the partially opened door, startling herself. She found that she was afraid of being seen, that someone had witnessed what had happened and was judging her for it. Turning around, putting the body behind her, Mercy pulled the door the rest of the way open and slid outside.

Without thought she moved through the house, back toward the window where she had come in. The boards were still on the ground from Ella's intrusion. Mercy drifted over to the window and climbed out. It was like she was riding along in her own body again, simply observing as she headed toward the forest.

Her direction was aimless. Uniform trees and bushes passed by her, none of them given a second thought.

How could she explain this to anyone? How could she tell Kenny that she had murdered Ella and still expect him to love her? She would be hated. Even if the courts deemed it self-defense, which it wasn't, not really, her life would be ruined. No one would look at her the same way again. She would forever be cast as a murderer.

As her thoughts swirled around in despair, Mercy stumbled into a clearing in the woods. A pair of railroad tracks sliced their way through the trees and scrub. The tracks had been abandoned, just like the houses. Weeds, grass, and wild flowers grew up between the ties. The metal rails were beginning to rust while the trees overhead spread their branches, trying to take back the space that had been denied them. Mercy followed the rails for a bit, until she came across a road that bisected it.

The road was made of dirt and had been washed away from the rails, leaving them jutting up as hard bumps. The road wasn't maintained at all—ferns crowded around the edges—but tracks in the dirt suggested it had been recently used. Mercy figured that this must be the road the men had driven in on, and the two hard bumps she had felt were the train rails.

She looked up the road on the opposite side of the rails. It could hardly be called a road up that way. Whatever rain storms had washed away the dirt from around the rails, had also washed away most of everything else. Just rough, wild grass grew, with a set of tire tracks slicing through it. The tire tracks led up to another road, however. This one was paved, if not a little beaten up. This was most certainly the road she had come in on.

That paved snake would lead her back to civilization eventually; all she had to do was follow it. She could just walk along beside it, hide in the woods if the truck came, or stick her thumb out if anyone else showed up.

Civilization. Mercy had killed an innocent woman. Where was her place in society?

Snap.

Reacting fast, Mercy quickly hid behind the nearest tree. She peered out from around the bark toward where the branch had broken. It took a moment to spot him, but Mercy saw Reedus in another section of the woods. His mask was up on the top of his head and he stood perfectly still, his eyes wild and darting. He was afraid that someone had heard the snapping of the wayward branch he had just stepped on. Mercy knew the feeling intimately. He began walking through the trees again, going slowly, constantly alert. He wasn't heading for the road, but away from it, like he had just come from there. Maybe he was doubling back the way Mercy had in the woods outside her parents' home.

Mercy looked at the road. She then looked at Reedus. There was the path to her freedom. Here was the man who, through deceitful action, had taken away her freedom.

Reedus had caused Mercy to become a murderer, so now Mercy was going to show him her new-found skill. She stepped out from behind her tree. No longer was she the prey.

CHAPTER EIGHTEEN

IN LESS THAN TWELVE hours, Mercy had learned more about travelling silently than she had ever thought she could know. As she stalked Reedus through the woods, she knew all the best places to put her feet. She even kept near large trees and bushes, so that when Reedus looked around, there was a place for her to hide. And she somehow always knew when he was going to look around. Perhaps because they were the times that she would do the same. Even the route he took was similar to that of Mercy's during her midnight flight.

They weren't heading back toward the house. Mercy wasn't sure where they were going, but it wasn't to the house. She suspected Reedus was heading to a different home on the lake, although he avoided the open spaces of the houses they passed. At least three times now, he had paused, listened, and hurried across the open slash of a driveway. Mercy followed every time, unconcerned about being seen by others, only focusing on the man ahead. The irony that he was the one who wore the rabbit mask was not lost on her.

Mercy wondered about how she would kill him. She was so full of rage that the thought didn't faze her in the slightest. She had no weapons on her, and it was unlikely that he had any on him. If they went into one of the homes, maybe she could grab something from inside. If not, a large stick or a rock would do. Reedus was the smallest of the men. Without her knee injury, Mercy would have been well-matched against him. With the injury, however, the one he knew all about, she would need a plan. She needed a weapon, a method of taking him down.

She thought of nothing outside of killing Reedus. She didn't think of Kenny. She didn't think of Roofus. Her mother and father didn't once pass through her mind. She didn't picture her sister, away at school, studying to be an actress. Never was she concerned for little Robin, who was likely still in the hospital with his parents hovering nervously nearby. She thought only of Reedus. Of Reedus and the consequences he had set in motion. If only he had listened to the other men and stayed away from the hospital, none of this would have happened. He should have just stayed at home. He should never have signed away Max's kidney so callously. He should have seen this coming.

On and on they walked, one following the other. Whenever Mercy got a chance, she peered through the trees at the lake. She guessed they were nearly at the exact opposite end from where the house in which she had been held was situated.

Reedus finally stopped walking. He stood hunched over just up ahead, listening and looking all around. Mercy crouched down, peering through the jagged branches of a prickly bush. Reedus paused for a longer period of time than all the other times he had stopped. He was being extra careful, searching in every direction.

For quite awhile Mercy was within his line of sight. She stayed completely still, knowing that any movement would reveal her position. It was possible that Reedus saw her anyway. He may have spotted her and thought nothing of it, thinking that he had just stumbled upon her own hiding place. Whether she had been seen by him or not, Reedus didn't react to her presence. Once the area was thoroughly scanned, he stepped forward again.

Mercy followed at a greater distance than she had previously. Reedus was spooked, and she didn't want to risk giving away her intentions. Surprise was the best thing she had going for her.

She reached the spot where Reedus had stood and scanned the area. It was next to a large open space. All around was the patchy grass that Mercy had come to associate with the area. In the middle stood one of the homes, although it was in far worse shape than the others. The entire second floor had collapsed, scattering debris all around. The ground floor still stood, although it had clearly suffered damage from the floor above it. Through broken windows, Mercy could see that the bottom floor was filled with debris from the collapse. She couldn't see any way in which Reedus would be inside. She also couldn't see him anywhere else.

Shit, had she lost him? She regretted keeping her distance now. Mercy searched frantically for any place he could have gone. Was he on the other side of the building perhaps?

A rabbit—a real one—suddenly appeared next to the house, running like a shot for the woods. Mercy watched it, confused. She couldn't see where it had come from; it had just appeared next to the middle of the wall. Risking the open ground, Mercy headed toward the house, aiming for the spot from which the rabbit had appeared. There, she found a large hole in the ground. It looked like it might have once been a window well into a basement, but now was just a dirt slide into a dark slot under the house.

Mercy lay on her stomach alongside the hole and slowly stuck her head inside. It was dark and hard to make out anything clearly. She waited for her vision to adjust to the gloom. The dirt created a gentle slope all the way down to the concrete floor. The angle she was on didn't provide her a very good view of the basement. That, combined with the gloom, resulted in her not even being able to make out the dimensions of the space.

A soft, unidentifiable noise came from the hole. Reedus must be down there; she didn't know where else he could have gone. She maneuvered herself so that her legs rested on the dirt slope. It felt solid enough. Scuttling on her hands and feet like a crab, Mercy started her way down into the basement. She passed by a hole in the dirt that she suspected was the rabbit's den. She also passed by a few stones, one of which was egg-shaped, smooth, and about the size of a baseball. Mercy pried the stone out and tested it in her hand. It wouldn't make the best weapon, but it would do.

At the bottom of the slope, she stood on the solid cement floor. Reedus hadn't pounced on her from the darkness, so he must not have noticed her descent. Or he wasn't down there. Her eyes adjusted to the dark. The room wasn't nearly as large as she had imagined it would be. Pipes sticking out of the walls suggested the space had once held a boiler that had been removed. If the boiler had still been in there, there wouldn't have been much room left for Mercy. In the corner opposite the pipes, was a hallway. Mercy sidled over to it and looked down.

The hallway seemed to be the entire length of the house above, terminating in a staircase with broken steps. A glass-less window had heavy boards nailed to the outside of it, but a tiny gap let in a single sliver of light. It was just enough for Mercy to make out the space, including a pair of doors along the opposite side. One door, the one closest to her, was open, while the other was shut tight. She approached the open door.

No light or sound came from within. As Mercy got close enough to see inside, she made out a small space with pipes and a large, cracked mirror hanging crookedly on the wall. This had probably been a bathroom at some point in time. That left the closed door.

Odds were that Reedus was behind it. Mercy crept up on the door and pressed her ear to it. She wasn't sure if she actually heard anything or if her mind was just making it up. Easing herself to the ground, being gentle about her knee, Mercy lay so that she was right up against the crack at the bottom of the door. She pressed her eye up against it, just like she used to do when she was a child and wanted to spy on one of her siblings.

Her worries about being in the wrong place were erased. Reedus was, in fact, in the room, with a small flashlight in his hand. He shone the light ahead of him, his back to the door, focused on a table in front of him. Mercy couldn't tell what he was doing from her low angle.

Rising to her feet, Mercy gripped her rock tightly. She took hold of the doorknob with her left hand and turned it as slowly as she could. Once the latch had completely retreated into the door, she pushed on it. The door swung easily and, amazingly, silently. There was now nothing between Mercy and Reedus, and his back was to her.

Mercy had to concentrate to keep her breathing from getting out of control. There was nothing she could do about the heavy thudding of her heart, but so far, Reedus had somehow not heard it. Her rib cage was a better muffler than she had believed it to be.

Here was the man who had caused everything. Through his one action, he had knocked over the dominos that had started all of this, and through his cowardice in failing to mention it, he had dragged Mercy in as well. Reedus didn't look hurt; he had faired better than Mercy had during his flight. This enraged her further. It also looked like he was packing a bag with supplies. Apparently he had suspected he would be caught eventually, and had set up this house with get-away gear. It made Mercy see red.

Clatter, clatter, clack.

Loose rocks and dirt rolled down the dirt pile. Reedus heard the sound and turned. Mercy saw everything as though it were happening in slow motion. Reedus turned, holding a passport in one hand, his other wrapped around one of the straps of the backpack sitting on the table. The flashlight was on a string around his neck, the light casting strange shadows on his face. As he saw Mercy standing there, his eyes widened with surprise.

Mercy sprang. She brought forward her right hand, tightly wrapped around the stone, in a fast jab aimed at his temple. She connected, his head rocking back, with the mask just managing to cling to the top of it. He immediately reacted, much faster than Mercy had expected. Reedus swung the backpack around and hit her shoulder with it. She was thrown to one side. As she stumbled, trying to regain her balance, he stepped toward her, swinging the bag again. Mercy raised her arms to protect her head, but at the last moment, he swung low, hitting her bad knee. Blinding pain shot up through her leg, but she was silent as she toppled over.

So this was it. She was down, her knee felt as though it were on fire, and Reedus was above her. He was going to pummel her to death;

a few strong kicks to the head would do it. But he didn't. Mercy blinked in surprise as he turned and ran out of the room. Not wasting a moment, she scrambled up onto her feet, nearly fell over again thanks to her knee, and then stumbled after him.

She half hobbled, half ran down the hall. When Reedus came into sight, he was climbing the dirt hill. The stone was still in Mercy's hands. With all her might, she threw it as though it were a baseball. She had never been much of a ball player herself, but she had developed a mean pitch by helping her brother learn to bat better. Although this had been a long time ago, Mercy's muscles drew forth the memory. The stone whizzed through the air and connected with Reedus's head. He went down hard, face first into the dirt. Mercy continued to stagger closer.

Reedus scrambled up to his feet, abandoning his backpack that had slid to the bottom of the mound. His mask had also finally been knocked off, and was left in the dirt. He crawled for the opening above him.

When Mercy reached the hill she crawled up after him, her hands clawing at the dirt and rocks for purchase. As she passed the rabbit mask, she noticed a few drops of blood on it. So she had managed to make him bleed, at least a little bit. Good.

After she pulled herself through the opening and back out into sunlight, Mercy grabbed another rock. This one wasn't smooth and was oddly shaped, but she could carry it with one hand. She got to her feet, damning her knee and trying to ignore it. Reedus was running for the water.

Mercy ran after him. Every time her foot hit the ground she wanted to shriek, but she managed to save her breath through sheer will power alone. She was focused entirely on Reedus. Nothing else mattered.

Ahead of Reedus was a dock in better shape than the house. Next to that dock, where it met the shore, a ratty tarp fluttered in a weak breeze. It was toward the tarp that Reedus was running. It took a few strides, but Mercy realized there must be something under that tarp, some sort of boat. Reedus planned to jump into the boat and motor away up the river that fed out of the lake next to the house.

Mercy threw the rock. It didn't fly as true as the first one had. The rock missed Reedus by inches, whizzing past his ear. It landed in the water with a splash, quickly sinking to the bottom. Reedus glanced back at his pursuer, checking to see how close she was and whether she had any more rocks. In the process, he had stopped watching where he was going. His foot landed wrong, twisted painfully, and spilled him over. He toppled head over heels, until he splashed into the shallow water.

Reedus sprang back up to his feet as fast as he could, but the time he was down was long enough for Mercy to catch up. He stood, water dripping from his face and briefly blinding him. For the first time in Mercy's life, she roared. She roared as she leapt at Reedus, her head down like she was playing football. Reedus let out a *woof* of air as her bony shoulder connected with his stomach. They both went down into the stagnant lake.

Mercy was on top of him. The water was shallow, and smelled putrid, but that didn't matter. She perched on his shoulders, all her weight pinning him down. Her hands grabbed his face, holding that down too. Reedus thrashed beneath her. He attempted to roll, to buck, to pull away, but the mud that made up the lake-bed offered him no purchase, and hindered his efforts. All he did was kick up silt that obscured his face from Mercy's view. He changed tactics. His arms shot up out of the water, and he flailed, trying to punch her. He couldn't see, or get an angle that gave him a good enough shot. Although his blows were bruising Mercy, she held on. Reedus started to claw at her arms, leaving red furrows and drawing blood once or twice. When that didn't work, he shot his arms between Mercy's and attempted to pry them apart, but that just had the effect of Mercy digging her fingers more painfully into the flesh of his face.

Reedus was desperate. He became stronger as he tried to get away, to get air, but his efforts became more frantic. If he had been as coordinated as he had been earlier, that sudden strength would have been able to throw Mercy, but as it was, she was able to cling on. She wasn't even aware that she was screaming wordlessly at him.

He stopped moving. Was he dead? Mercy couldn't be sure. She continued to sit on him, and hold his face down. After a few seconds, Reedus's whole body began to shudder and convulse under her weight. He spasmed and shook and tremored. There was no coordination at all to these movements, no thought behind them. This was his body's last attempt to get air, its final desperate plea, an automatic response. Just as suddenly as he started, Reedus stopped moving again.

Mercy stayed on top of him, not ready to get off yet. She stayed there a long time, watching the silt settle, his features slowly reappearing. The dirt gathered on his face, in the hollows of his eyes, in his nose, in his mouth.

It was harder for Mercy to believe that she had killed him than it was to believe that she had killed Ella. Here was one of her tormentors, a man who had changed her life permanently. And yet he died, just like everyone else.

The old Mercy was gone. In this dead lake, a new Mercy was born.

CHAPTER NINETEEN

"It's been at least ten minutes, I'm quite sure he's dead."

Mercy sprang to her feet and turned, finally setting free Reedus's body so it could slowly bob to the surface. The bird was standing on the shore, his mask over his upper face again. Mercy searched around for a weapon, anything with which she could defend herself. The bird raised his hands, showing Mercy that he was unarmed, actually trying to make her less frightened. It didn't work, but Mercy did stop searching, if only because she could see there was nothing within immediate reach.

"I have no plans to harm you, Mercy," the bird said. "Not unless you have plans to harm me."

Mercy just watched him, watching every tiny movement he made.

"You killed my brother."

No response.

"That's okay. Although we could have used him to find Father's kidney, we don't mind that you killed him."

At the mention of 'we' Mercy's eyes darted past the bird. She scanned the house and trees, quickly locating where the rat, the cat, and the snake stood. They all wore their masks. Max was with them, sitting serenely in his wheelchair.

"He would like to talk to you."

"Your father?" Mercy finally spoke. Her voice sounded different to her own ears. Perhaps it was from all the roaring and screaming.

"Yes. Our father. Maxime Fowler, as you know him. He could be your father too."

Mercy frowned.

"Please. Come." The bird stepped closer and held out his hand.

After a moment of thought, Mercy took it. The bird helped her out of the lake, the mud sucking at her shoes. She slid her hand out of his the moment she was on solid ground. They walked up the hill together, Mercy a step behind the bird, her eyes seeking out weapons and escape routes the entire time.

"Mercy." Max smiled at her as she got close.

The bird joined the other masked men standing behind Max. Mercy stood before the group, ready to flee at the first sign of trouble. Her eyes darted from one to the other, watching them carefully.

"I knew I saw potential in you," Max said to her. When she didn't answer he continued. "We always knew that Reedus had this hideout here. We didn't know why he thought he needed it, but the fact that he thought he could keep it from us brought some amusement. While Jacob chased him through the woods, Patel came straight here to wait for him."

Mercy's eyes flicked from the cat to the snake. They had both run out the door after Reedus.

"Jacob," Max pointed at the cat, "and Patel," he pointed at the snake. "Patel watched him go in and was about to follow, but can you imagine his surprise when you came out of the woods? Bret, here," pointing at the bird "had been following you all along. He was less surprised when you went stalking after Reedus. Tell me, what was it like for you to kill Ella?"

Mercy didn't respond.

"Bret watched you go into the house. He watched Ella go in awhile later. You came out alone, with blood on you. Naturally, we assume you killed her."

Mercy nodded once.

"Wonderful! So unexpected." Max was actually excited, clapping his hands once. The other men stayed perfectly still. "And even after that, you hunted down and killed Reedus. I am so proud of you."

"You're proud of me because I killed your son?" Mercy found that extremely strange, bordering on sick.

"I'm proud of you because you learned to adapt. You learned to change. It's regrettable that my son had to die, but I have five other sons. To watch a beautiful new creation being born is certainly worth it."

"Are you going to let me go?" Mercy was tired of his odd ramblings.

"You're free to go wherever you wish," Max told her, waving his arm at everything around them. "Although I don't know where you would go."

"Home."

"And where is that? That apartment you share with that cop? You really think you can go there? Mercy, Mercy, Mercy. You killed a woman. Probably accidental manslaughter, yes, but you did kill her. And Reedus. That, I know, was just flat out murder. No way you can claim self-defense on that one." He tapped a finger against a video camera sitting on his lap. Did Max have a recording of the killing?

Mercy shifted her weight from her good leg to her bad leg, and then quickly back again.

"You can't go back to your life, Mercy."

Mercy finally looked away from them, glancing at the ground beneath her feet. She knew she couldn't go back to her life. There was no way she could just be Mercy Chalmers anymore, a nurse in a coma ward who lived with her boyfriend and dog, and who went to see her parents every weekend. That life was gone. It was just a framework of dust and cobwebs in her mind now.

"I can offer you a place to stay."

Mercy looked up, her eyes fiery.

"You may have noticed that none of my sons look very much alike, or like me for that matter. They are not my sons through birth. I adopted them. All of them, when they were homeless like you. Each of them needed a place to go after their life was shattered."

Mercy studied each of the men. She tried to see those lives beyond the masks. Looking into their eyes, she saw something familiar in each of them. She saw something she felt growing inside herself.

"You want to adopt me?"

"Yes! I always wanted a daughter, but no one ever lived up to my dreams. You, Mercy, you are special."

"What about the wolf?"

"You mean Christian. He's very upset with you, but he shouldn't be. He should be upset with himself for losing. I can set him straight. Or I'll let you kill him if you'd like. What do you say, Mercy?"

Max held out a hand. From his fingers hung Reedus's rabbit mask.

Mercy stepped forward. She took the mask from him and looked it over. It was dirty, and Reedus's blood was still on it. The rubber was soft, and the elastic tight. She returned her attention to the men standing before her. None of them moved. She looked at the trees around her. She looked at the lake behind her. She looked at the house. The rabbit that had been scared out of its home was now making its way along the side of the building, heading back toward its hole.

She turned to face the men once more. She placed the mask over her face, peering out through the eyeholes and wrapping the elastic around the back of her head. The inside of the mask smelled pleasant.

"What do I have to do?"

CHAPTER TWENTY

BY THE TIME STANLEY got home, he was soaked with sweat. It had been a scorching summer day, but still he had insisted on going for a run. He enjoyed running.

After a quick shower and a change of clothes, he sat on his couch and put his feet up. Later that day, he had a date with the delicious Lucinda, but for now, he had time to kick back and watch the game. His favourite baseball team was playing.

During the commercial breaks, Stanley flipped channels. He couldn't stand to watch the advertisements. He saw them in the same way as he saw telemarketers: nothing but a nuisance.

"-Baby, I love you," said a man in a soap opera.

Click.

"-and if you buy-"

Click.

A laugh track.

Click.

"-shed new light on the case-"

Click.

Wait, that was the news. Stanley had no problem with the news, especially considering that he was a photographer for the local paper. He flipped back to the previous channel, cutting off some overly cute kid's cartoon.

"-la Rodriguez." Stanley recognized the Rodriguez name along with the picture they were showing of a smiling woman. They were talking about a high profile case that had started two months ago when two women went missing. One of the women's parents' home, where the woman had been staying, was found broken into, the place a mess, and their neighbours slaughtered. There was security footage of the other woman, the Rodriguez woman, being kidnapped in a parking garage and driven off in a truck.

"Early yesterday, Mercy Chalmers was reportedly seen back at Callus General Hospital, where she was employed as a nurse," said the reporter. "Although the police haven't released much information on the sighting, security footage suggests that she was alone. Police are asking anyone who sees her, to contact them, as she is wanted for questioning in this brutal case." The picture of Ella Rodriguez was replaced by one of Mercy Chalmers, as well as a number to call.

Stanley had been following the story with interest. He wouldn't say he followed it closely, but he tried to pick up new information whenever it was released. A few weeks after the women had gone missing, an unidentified man's body was found floating in a river. He had been dead for awhile, drowned. In an attempt to find out where and how he had drowned, police had wound up finding the body of Ella Rodriguez instead. If the drowned man and she were related, the police weren't saying. The whole lake was off-limits as the police had apparently found something else there that they didn't want contaminated.

Since then, everything about the case had gone quiet. The police were getting nowhere, and things weren't looking good for the Chalmers woman. Now, though, with what Stanley had just heard, things were getting interesting again. What was the Chalmers woman doing? If she had been kidnapped, why hadn't she talked to anyone about it? She was alone at the hospital? That seemed strange. And why was she there to begin with?

The news report ended, with nothing more than the same questions Stanley was asking. No doubt the Chalmers family would be harassed by reporters again. Because Mr. Chalmers had won an Academy award, he had lately been the focus of many reporters' badgering.

Stanley often wondered if the case would have gotten so much attention if he weren't linked to it.

Stanley flipped back to the baseball game, the commercials having ended. It didn't take long before he forgot all about the news report.

Just after the game ended, with Stanley's team beating the other guys by a close two runs, his phone started ringing. He checked the call display and saw that it was an unknown name with an unknown number. Usually he didn't pick up such calls, but he was in a good mood, and it might be one of his friends calling to talk about the game.

"Hello?"

"Is this Stanley Kirkman?" a pleasant female voice asked him.

"Yes it is." Inwardly, Stanley groaned, thinking that he had picked up a telemarketer.

"This is Ms. Fowler, I'm calling from the Musket General Hospital. Do you have a few minutes?"

"What's this about?" Stanley sat up straighter, wondering why the hospital was calling him.

"It's nothing urgent, sir. The hospital has been doing some re-organizing lately, and your name came up on a list of patients from a few years ago. We were hoping we could ask you a few questions about your stay with us. Anything you tell us will be kept strictly confidential and will help us improve service for future patients."

Stanley was relieved it was just a survey. Normally he would just hang up on survey takers, but this was the hospital. He had been treated well there and would like to help out if he could. "Sure, fire away."

"Wonderful, thank you. Now, our records show you were here for a transplant?"

"That's right. A kidney."

ABOUT THE AUTHOR

Kristal Stittle was born and raised in Toronto, where she continues to live for most of the year. During the summer, she can be found around the woods and lakes of Muskoka, a favoured place by both her and her cat.

She writes in all genres, and while she focuses on novels and short stories most of the time, she also dabbles with film scripts. A graduate of Humber College, trained as a 3D artist, she still enjoys painting as well as photography. Before actualizing her dream as an author, Kristal worked at both Blockbuster and Ubisoft, which appealed to her film and video game loving sides. You can frequently find her on Twitter @kristalstittle.

www.ingramcontent.com/pod-product-compliance
Lightning Source LLC
Chambersburg PA
CBHW051230210726
48290CB00003B/888